'Unsparing and .... rs through the landscape of the .... ndour and humour that will make Caragh Maxwell's voice ..mmediately known.'

ANNE ENRIGHT, author of *The Wren, The Wren*

'*Sugartown* is a very real and penetrating account of modern Ireland, and of one woman's struggle to escape the somatic pain that she reels in. I have never felt quite so unsettled and immersed in a narrative. Deeply affecting and startlingly real, this unsettling fiction delves into loss, loneliness, the complication of blended families, addiction and growing up in Ireland with an originality that is refreshing and terrifying. A gut punch of a rollicking ride.'

ELAINE FEENEY, author of *How to Build a Boat*

'Caragh Maxwell's debut novel *Sugartown* captures the zeitgeist of a generation coming of age in post-boom Ireland, not in Trinity College but in a stagnant town with limited prospects. The prose is exquisite; the narrative beats with the thrum of the bass then devastates in tender heartbreaking moments. Utterly compelling, authentic and raw, this an astonishing debut and Caragh Maxwell's voice is one we should be hearing.'

UNA MANNION, author of *Tell Me What I Am*

'For all the grit and heartbreak of *Sugartown*'s landscape, Caragh Maxwell is a subtle writer and her authority as a stylist is lightly worn. The prose is exquisite, understated, yet blazes with insight in a way that few writers can achieve. Maxwell is the most naturally gifted young writer of her generation and *Sugartown* is a stunning debut.'

EOIN McNAMEE, author of *The Bureau*

sugartown

caragh maxwell

ONEWORLD

A Oneworld Book

First published in the United Kingdom, Republic of Ireland
and Australia by Oneworld Publications Ltd, 2025

ISBN 978-1-83643-100-8
eISBN 978-1-83643-102-2

Printed and bound in Great Britain by Clays Ltd, Elcograf S.p.A

This book is a work of fiction. Names, characters, businesses,
organisations, places and events are either the product of the author's
imagination or are used fictitiously. Any resemblance to actual persons,
living or dead, events or locales is entirely coincidental.

The authorised representative in the EEA is eucomply OÜ,
Pärnu mnt 139b–14, 11317 Tallinn, Estonia
(email: hello@eucompliancepartner.com / phone: +33757690241)

Oneworld Publications Ltd
10 Bloomsbury Street
London WC1B 3SR
England

Stay up to date with the latest books,
special offers, and exclusive content from
Oneworld with our newsletter

Sign up on our website
oneworld-publications.com

MIX
Paper | Supporting
responsible forestry
FSC® C018072

To all the Mullingar girls – don't stop.

I

No one came to collect me from the airport. I took the express bus from Dublin all the way to town and then used the last twenty available on my debit card to get out to my mother's house, hidden up a side road on the outskirts of civilisation, heaving with bags, breathless by the time I wrestled them from the boot of the taxi. The driver tried to lend a hand and I waved him off, distrust motivating me, burning my cheeks scarlet as I fumbled with the heft of my big suitcase. He'd had to drop me at the end of the road; the meter was climbing and I stopped him at eighteen, petrified it'd tip past twenty and I'd have to ask someone in the house to cover the rest. Also, he gave off bad vibes and I didn't want him to know exactly which house I lived in. Surreptitiously, while pretending – poorly, I was no actress – to take a selfie, I'd snapped a photo of his driver badge and made a note of his car brand and registration number and sent it to Doireann, my best friend. *If I go missing this was the taxi I was in xoxo.* She gave my message a thumbs up and I felt a little better. The driver asked me several times if I'd be okay waiting there on the side of the unlit road as the sky darkened, did I have someone coming to meet me? I reassured him yes; I even pretended to take a phone call from my concerned father, hoping it'd scare him back into the taxi. He peeled out of the ditch slowly, and I could see him watching me in the wing mirror as he got ready to re-enter the main road. I kept a polite smile plastered to my face until he was out of sight, my blood pressure drumming underneath my collarbones, a sheen of sweat breaking on the back of my neck. Then, I gathered up my bags, popped the handle on my suitcase, and started the ascent of the big hill, the suitcase wheels catching on the loose gravel constantly, skittering pebbles against my heels.

I tried to play out my next hour and my walk slowed with every passing scenario. My mother, instantly hennish and gesticulating; JJ, as quiet and country as ever; my sisters, a big fat question mark because I didn't really know them at all. I hadn't seen my sisters in five years and I doubted they remembered me as more than a peach-coloured blob-person in the background of a faint toddler memory. Lily, who was three at the time, might have been able to recall the shape of my face, the sound of my voice. Emilia knew about ten words when I left and none of them were *Saoirse*. I'd never even met Gracie, who'd been kicking Máire in the bladder as I boarded the flight to London. They were eight, six and five respectively now. My mother had been so miserable raising me that I assumed she'd never wanted children in the first place, but I was wrong. The way she doted on them was almost sickening. She did the *Baby's First...* books with each of them, immortalising them with handwritten memories of the birthing process, first bottle feeds, first tastes of solid foods, a lock of hair from their first haircuts pressed lovingly between the thick, stiff pages, their first baby booties pinned to the back cover. I thumbed through Lily's once and spent a week in bed afterwards. I didn't know why at the time. Before I muted her account, Máire's Facebook was like a shrine to them; all three lined up on church steps or a bench at Dublin Zoo or on a towel on a French beach, dressed in subtly matching outfits – she'd never be so tacky as to buy them all the same – with captions about how these days were the best days. About how being a mother changed her life for the better. About how Lily's spelling was MENSA-level impressive, how Emilia's Irish dancing skills would have her front-row one-two-threeing for Michael Flatley one day, how Gracie's ability to spoon-feed herself mashed potato would put Gordon Ramsay to shame. It was just me she didn't want.

I hadn't expected Máire to be home; when I told her my arrival time she'd sighed and hummed and hawed and threatened to move things around so she could pick me up, and instead of reducing myself to begging I said I'd make my own way back. She broke through the Venetian blinds when I knocked on the front door, lifting the gaudy, heavy brass knocker shaped like the tail of a fox hanging from the mouth of a beagle. It was disgusting. James would've reeled back until his chin disappeared into his neck and his upper lip hit his nostrils, militant in his PETA-brand veganism. I used to find this level of passion alluring. Now I was just sad for all the rashers I'd refused to eat over the previous three years and embarrassed that I'd said nothing when he compared dairy farming to the Holocaust in front of our coworkers in the pub. My opinion of him had rapidly lost opacity until it was glassless and I could see him, watching me squat on my suitcase and wrestle with the zip, offering no help, and I could *see* him. I could see the last half-decade of my life squashed up and thrown on the ground like a cigarette butt, stepped on by his battered black Converse. I bought sausage rolls while I waited for my flight back home and devoured them. The pink Play-Doh meat oozed out from between the yellow, crusty pastry, and my insides flipped but I kept eating, one after another, until my lips were greasy and my tongue was thick. I vomited them back up mid-flight and, once the nausea settled, blocked and deleted James on every social media account I had.

Máire, my mother, answered the door in a swoop, the winged arms of her patterned kaftan gracefully floating to her sides, her blonde hair coiffed and piled to deliberately look effortless and messy. She was so swift that the blinds were still shivering as she went to hug me. I awkwardly let my carry-on bag fall to my hip to accept; the smell of hairspray, bleach, and expensive perfume was a time machine. I wanted to be five years old again. I wanted to be held and soothed and tucked into bed. My bones felt like splintered bamboo, weakened and bendy. I'd left the flat for the last time at half four that morning and hadn't stopped since; I was tired, and probably heartbroken. She pulled away, and I had to catch myself from stumbling. The minute I stepped across the threshold I knew I'd come on the wrong week. It was the very worst week of the year to be living with my mother, beating out Christmas week by a country mile. It was the week of The Great Spring Clean.

The Great Spring Clean was an annual ritual in my mother's house; it usually took the guts of seven days and fell conspicuously across the Easter midterm every single year. God help you if you were spotted with idle hands. Husbands, children, and visitors alike were armed with rubber gloves, dusting cloths, Pledge cans, bin bags, and a list of tasks to be done. Generally, you were instructed to start in your own bedroom and work your way around to the common areas, and at the end of each day, it gave Máire visible pleasure to survey the work done. Each bedroom, in her opinion, needed a bin bag full of donations and a bin bag full of rubbish and if these weren't produced, she'd come into the room with you and start throwing away things that she deemed no longer fit for use. More than once I'd hidden jeans, cardigans, teddy bears, books, and other favourite items at my Granny Maher's house until the purge was over and it was safe to bring them home again. It was probably the one week of the year that, even in all the throes of teenage angst and ire, I would quietly obey my mother. The Great Spring Clean was something she *had* to do. She couldn't bypass it, couldn't reset herself until every ounce of clutter and cobweb had been banished to the wheelie bins. It was like witnessing a blood-frenzied snake shed its skin. The year my father moved out she even hired a skip and threw out armchairs, dinner plates, mattresses, lampshades, anything he'd ever liked or slept on or eaten off or touched. That time I'd scavenged a large flannel shirt of his, a photo of the three of us in the hospital the day I was born, and a Harp pint glass he used to drink two fizzy vitamin C tablets out of every morning. All three items had made the journey to and from London with me; the photo was pressed between the battered pages of *The Great Gatsby*, my favourite book, and the pint glass was wrapped in the flannel shirt to stop it from shattering. I didn't tell him I was coming home. I did try to, once or twice, pulled up his number, hit call and then immediately hung up, typed out a text and deleted it again. It had been nearly a year since I'd heard from him, one of the longer stretches we'd gone without speaking. I always called eventually, guilty and sad. I guess I wanted him to look for me first this time. I couldn't ask Máire what to do. She would have preferred to forget he ever existed at all. But there I was, every day, the slope of my nose and the jut of my chin reminding her.

It was a Thursday, so Máire was through the worst of it. By then, she was usually replacing all the furniture she'd pulled apart, putting tables back in their corners, cushions back on their sofas, curtains back on their rails, all hoovered, dusted, laundered, pressed. The wardrobes and cupboards would all have a little echo in them, their contents significantly thinned and scented with Febreze. I picked my suitcase up and placed it gently on the hardwood floor, conscious of marking it and starting off on the wrong foot. The hallway windows were bare and stretched from floor to ceiling, illuminating all the steps of the big pine staircase that led up to an open-sided landing, off which sprung door after door. It was like stepping into a show home or a sitcom set. Signs of humanity were minimal but visible; a bucket of water and vinegar next to a sweeping brush with a squeegee masking-taped to the handle. A wall with an assortment of family photos, one of which, I was surprised to see, was a school photo of mine from when I was about seven. An IKEA coat rack mounted to the wall, shrouded in pink vinyl jackets and hi-vis vests and bike helmets and what seemed like dozens of scarves – but even this had order, organisation, my mother written all over it.

—No shoes in the house, pet, I just had the floors done.

I nodded and pried my boots off one by one, leaving them together outside the front door. She took a breath then, and her tight smile relaxed into something closer to real.

—Come on into the kitchen and I'll pop on the kettle.

The kitchen was less put-together, but this wasn't unusual; it followed the pattern. Bedrooms, bathrooms, hallways, kitchen, living room. Baskets of delft and glass and cutlery sat out on the kitchen island, all in neat stacks, ready to be inspected for viability. Already she had a box on the floor for the charity shop containing plastic toddler cups and bowls, and another box for the bin containing chipped mugs and scratched silverware; stuff not fit for anyone, in her opinion. Not even the needy. She made tea and I looked around. Two-door fridge-freezer, induction hob built into the counter, wood-burning stove, intricate mosaic backsplash, double-paned patio door, an actual patio beyond the door. She'd married up when she married JJ. This was not the house I thought of as *home*.

The house I still thought of as home was a cramped, damp bungalow named Hill Lodge by the landlord who also happened to be my auntie's husband; assurance that we wouldn't be turfed out. It had three bedrooms and one bathroom and a tiny patch of scrub garden that bordered a field full of horses. I'd loved it. Then Máire had met her second husband. JJ was fine. He was thoughtful and masculine and had a good head on his shoulders. His family were nice people. He was twelve years older than my mother. He had a good job as a quarry foreman, a parcel of land outside of town, no kids, a bald spot, and a penchant for boot-cut jeans. Before he'd proposed to Máire, he'd asked me for my permission and I'd said yes because he made her happier and more stable than I'd ever seen her. She didn't take to the bed once after she'd met him. She stopped taking turns at starving herself or skipping showers, instead consistently remembering how to be a functioning human. She quit smoking cigarettes. She stopped waking me up and confiding her anxieties in me late at night. The trade-off was my own happiness. I was fourteen and dramatic. I was spending court-ordered weekends in my father's flat, the divorced-dad energy of the place sad and suffocating. I loved Hill Lodge. It was my Eden. I loved it so much that when my mother married JJ and started to build their dream home, I privately and sometimes publicly cursed them into the ground. We'd moved into Hill Lodge when I was eleven, my entire lifetime before had been spent hopping from grandmother's house to mouldy flat to other grandmother's house to piddly bedsit. My bedroom was a small rectangle with brown, pansy-shaped water stains on the walls and the ceiling that, no matter how many layers of purple paint we rolled on, would bleed back through again and again. I papered the moist plaster with hundreds of posters, Kurt Cobain and Eddie Vedder and Courtney Love and Chris Cornell, a shrine to a music genre rapidly approaching dad-rock and something I would grow out of once I moved away – although, on a bad day, my Spotify would look like the inset of a nineties grunge compilation album. Once, I put a deadbolt and padlock on either side of the door to stop my mother from snooping. She took a Black & Decker cordless drill to the screws the same day. By the time my bags had been packed for college, my mother and her new family were filling the last of the cardboard boxes to take to the new house. She would never assign me a new bedroom, and I would never ask for one.

I'd stayed in the guest room before, for a month. After I'd dropped out of college and gone a bit insane. Máire had to come get me from the student apartment I shared with Doireann. She'd had to pack up all my things for me as I was catatonic. She put me in the car and drove me back here. She ran me a bath and washed the weeks of bed-sweat off me, untangling the mats out of my hair with a gentle hand. She put me into this bed and made me tea and toast and scratched my back until I fell asleep. She never asked me what was wrong because she knew. She was fond of a depressive turn herself. She brought me to her GP who put me on antidepressants. I never took them. I booked a flight to London instead.

That evening, I sat at the kitchen table pushing lumpy, yellowed mashed potato around a plate while my stepfather asked me questions about London, and Lily, Emilia, and Gracie butted in every now and again to show or tell me something before being reprimanded by the ever-militant Máire, tea towel in one hand while the other pointed at her target in a threatening manner. She'd managed to cook a whole roast chicken and all the vegetables with about half a foot of free counter space, some of the glass-filled boxes stacked atop one another, just begging to be bumped into and smashed to bits. When JJ asked why I had to leave my apartment, my mother answered for me – *save that for another day*. I'd had to tell her the truth when I'd asked to move in here, knowing the humiliation would make me more pitiable. She put a hand, still clammy and warm from washing dishes, on the back of my neck in what I initially assumed was a comforting gesture. What followed was a swift and puncturing pain; she'd gripped a pimple on my hairline between her thumbnail and index finger, squeezing until it burst. I hissed and pulled away, slapping a sleeve-clad palm to the site of the pain. The pale blue wool came back with a pinprick of blood.

—Jesus Christ, Máire.

—You have to suffer to be beautiful. Anyway you'd never have seen it yourself. It was like a second skull emerging. You're welcome.

She was rubbing her hands together under the tap then, washing my detritus out from under the whorls of her fingerprints. I had a tissue up my sleeve, which I pressed to the back of my neck several times until the white stayed unsullied. I rinsed my plate and excused myself, climbing the stairs to their guest room, noting the steps that creaked.

The guest room was like something from a middle-class wet dream, and my bags, slumped against the foot of the mahogany bed frame, were akin to a dirty crisp packet in an otherwise crystalline block of ice. Máire had put all my things into storage, she informed me – really she'd just bagged it all and stuck it up in the attic, most likely taking the opportunity to throw away things of mine she'd never liked. I wasn't too hurt at the thought; if I'd really cared about any of it I would've brought it with me. I opened my big shell suitcase to dig out pyjamas, the lid slapping against the wood floor in a way that made me wince, and the smell of the apartment blossomed from thin air. Onions and garlic frying, pink Surf fabric softener, a little hint of damp from the bedroom wardrobe. It hurt to remember – the stiff curl of our cheap, overwashed bath mat under my bare feet, the dip in the mattress on my side, *Blonde* by Frank Ocean playing gently on James's record player while we smoked a joint in the semi-darkness, the lilt of his indistinct accent, rough from smoking, like honey and pepper.

I pulled on my pyjamas and shut the light off, crawled into the cool, white sheets, pulled medically taut to the mattress, and cried, quietly, as the state of my life came into focus. Just as sleep started to come, I heard someone climb the stairs, stop outside my door and put their hand on the handle, the weight of it making the metal squeak ever so slightly. Then I suppose they thought better of it and walked away.

———

A couple of days after I got back, my lamp was delivered. The postman, overly chatty, hands like shovels, was surprisingly gentle with the box.

—You're a new face. Friend of the family?

—No. Long-lost daughter.

I spent the next three minutes trying to disengage the box from his hands while he asked me all manner of questions; where was I before, what was I doing before, am I in college or what, and am I JJ's daughter or who sired me? That was the one that made me straighten my spine, grip the box with both hands and pull, thank him for the delivery and shut the door in his face.

In the kitchen, I slit the parcel tape open with a paring knife while my mother watched me from her perch against the cabinets.

—Get stuck talking to Kevin?

—Bit nosy, isn't he?

—And a mouth like Galway Bay. Did you do next-day delivery on something?

—No, it's my lamp I posted from England.

Carefully, I lifted it out, thick with a layer of bubble wrap, packing peanuts escaping the box and scattering themselves across the kitchen island. Máire watched as I unwrapped it, the ochres and crimsons and golds of the glass shade coming into view. Once freed, I twisted the brass-vined base around with one hand under the natural light from the window, making sure there were no scuffs, no dings, no cracks. It was perfect. The breath in my chest came loose and my shoulders relaxed. Máire's eyebrows were quirked.

—Where in the name of God did you dig that thing up from?

—Do ya not like it?

—It's as ugly as sin. Keep it in the room.

—That was the plan.

The guest room had a lamp on either side of the bed, bone-coloured porcelain cubes with rectangular shades that made the light too bright. I replaced the left-side one with my own one, stole its bulb to throw red tones against the dull ivory of the wall. The lamp did not blend into the room by any stretch of the imagination. Among the coolness of varying shades of cream, the sleek edges of the furniture, even the faux-rustic floorboards, it stuck out like a sore thumb wearing a sovereign ring. And I loved it. I loved it just as much as the day I bought it. I'd been worried that I'd get it back to Ireland and look at it and see only James, our apartment, the hallway table next to the coat hooks that held incense and keys and my lamp, always on past six o'clock in the evening, its uterine light comforting.

—So that's it then?

—Don't start, Saoirse.

—Don't start, Saoirse? Don't fucking start, Saoirse?

I wanted to be angry but already my face was wet with tears and my nose was beginning to run. Betrayed by my own secretions. James was maudlin-faced and stoic, his arms crossed against his chest so tight that I could see the flesh mottling as the blood flow was cut off. We were sitting across from each other, me on the sofa, sinking into the end with the broken box springs, him on the arm of the big leather armchair, my armchair, putting creases in the blanket underneath him.

—Look, you've a week to get yourself sorted. I'll stay somewhere else. But when I come back next Friday, you need to be gone.

—A week? Sure where in London do you expect me to find a place to live by next fucking Friday? What'll I do with all my stuff, all my furniture?

—Saoirse. Point to one piece of furniture in this room, in this entire flat, that you own.

I'd glanced around defiantly at first, and then a little desperately. Then I remembered. I stood up and crossed the room, into the cramped hallway, and picked up the lamp. I'd bought it out of the back of somebody's Ford Focus at a car boot sale the summer before. It was one of those imitation Tiffany stained-glass lamps, the nicotine-chic shade reminiscent of the old wallpaper in my Granny Maher's house. The base was wrought with brassy vines, ending here and there in a hardened, tarnished blossom. I'd paid the Focus driver fifteen pounds for it, taken it home and scrubbed it with Brasso and a baby toothbrush until it was gleaming. It was my favourite thing in the flat, probably, I now realised, because it was the only thing of mine on display. James's face remained stone when I re-entered the living room, sniffling and clutching the lamp like it was my newborn child, trying to set my own face in passivity despite my leaky eyes.

—You can keep it. I never really liked it anyway.

—Oh, how very generous of you to let me keep my own lamp. You're some fella, aren't you. Some fucking prick.

—Yeah, I'm always the prick, aren't I? Well if I have to be the prick, this is the last time.

—What's that supposed to mean?

But he didn't reply. He just sighed in that tone he took when I did something naive or stupid or otherwise displeasing, a tone he'd been building and perfecting over those last few months in particular. The end of our relationship wasn't exactly a shock, but I'd been living in dread all the same because it meant I'd have to leave. His parents owned the apartment. I never signed a lease because I was too shy to push for it and I really, really liked him. The roommates-to-lovers trope hit us hard; we snuck around behind the back of our third flatmate, snotty Helen the politics student who didn't like me because I put her cast iron pan in the dishwasher my first week there. I did replace the pan and bought her a bottle of wine to say sorry, but she never really let it go. The sneaking around made it better, more intense; we'd shag on the dining table, the sofa, in the tiny shower stall of the one bathroom we all shared, all of the common areas, whenever Helen was at work or class, and I took a secret glee in it when she was being a covert bitch to me. She moved out not long after we became official, and that's when we did the car boot sale run – to fill all the little chasms Helen's things left behind.

James could have afforded to live alone. He could have afforded to buy anything he liked for the flat. The house-mates and the car boot sale rummages were a deliberate choice. His parents may have owned the apartment but they didn't know he was subletting; he wanted to be independent of them, to make it on his own. So he pocketed mine and Helen's rent each month and spent it mostly on ketamine and vinyls. He'd never get caught because they didn't care to visit him. We'd bonded over that initially. The mutual heartsickness of parental alienation is responsible for many terrible relationships.

The lamp was making me feel a bit better about my situation. When I turned it on at night it was like wrapping myself in a big heated fleece. It made the room mine during the hours it was turned on, and by its light I re-read *Gatsby*, using the photo as a bookmark so every time I opened my page, my own blank baby face stared up at me from between my parents, younger than I was now, something inscrutable in their expressions.

I was owed one more wage from the pub and then I was destitute. I spent my first mornings back flicking through employment websites, cringing a little at the number of postings requiring a degree and more years of experience than I'd been an adult. Still, I threw a CV at anything I might have remotely had a shot at – secretary, bar manager, customer service expert, sales representative. Each posting required me not only to attach my CV but to painstakingly type up the details contained in the CV into neat little boxes with letter counts. I could only apply to two or three at a time before I felt the tension begin to grow in the tendons of my fingers. Then I'd shut the laptop and sidle downstairs, trying already to avoid my mother, whose skin I seemed to slip under so easily. She didn't even need to voice her annoyance; she'd just throw her eyes my way or place her cup on the glass-top table with a *chink* sound that made me bristle, and I'd stop to take stock of whatever it was I was doing, analyse it to see what it was that vexed her. Sometimes it'd be forgetting to turn the boiling kettle away from the wall so the steam didn't get trapped beneath the underside of the cabinet, or leaving the back door open for the dog while he did his business outside. Once, I'd singed popcorn in the microwave, and she'd sighed and slapped around the kitchen in mule slippers, dramatically throwing open the windows and doors while waving a dishcloth. I wondered what she thought about when she looked at me. What I made her think about.

The girls were, despite my mother's coolness and despite my own attempts to blend into the wallpaper, in awe of me.

They liked to loiter outside my bedroom door and pretend to play, hoping to catch a glimpse of me or stop me on my way out and ask me things like *do you like my nail polish I did myself?* before wiggling a little chubby hand at me, sparkly enamel smeared and dried all over the cuticles of the fingers. It was a struggle sometimes to be around them, to see how much Máire doted on them. Although I had at least a modicum of foresight, enough to know that this level of helicopter parenting would serve them no better as adults than her neuroticism had served me. As it was, they stepped on each other's necks to please her. If Emilia left her dirty socks kicked under the bed, Lily would run and tell Máire. If Lily fed her toast crusts to the dog under the table, Gracie would point and screech *Lily's feeding Max! You said not to and she's doing it!* There was no loyalty among them, no coven of little witches that might protect one another, encircle one another, keep one another's confidences. Sometimes I wanted to gather them around and teach them the importance of loyalty, of sisterhood, but who the fuck was I to impart sisterly wisdom when I was the least involved of all of us? Plus, our sizable age difference made it uncomfortable in a moral way. I wasn't going to be the creepo teaching kids how to keep secrets from adults. All I could do was look on and try to fit in around the weird matriarchal tenets Máire had built her household upon. But by God, did she make it difficult. For at least the first fortnight I felt like nothing short of a serf invited up to stay at the Big House by my generous, stately landlord while my wattle-and-daub hut was being reconstructed after a freak storm blew it to smithereens. I didn't know how to act around them, any of them.

They all seemed to run on a set track while I crossed back and forth, up and down, zig-zagging, sometimes throwing them off their course.

Máire worked as a GP's secretary part time; every morning, before nine, she got the girls up, dressed and off to the local primary school without fuss. On Thursdays and Fridays she busied herself with her hobbies; reefing weeds out of her flowerbeds, power-walking the back roads, going for a swim in the pool of the town's nicer hotel, taking herself to brunch, meal-prepping for the following week. The lack of fun in her schedule was palpable, but it kept her largely away from me, which meant less opportunity to bicker. The girls got up, went to school, came home, got in and had a healthy snack pre-prepped by Máire, sat at the table and did their homework, and fought like cats when Máire wasn't there. JJ's mother Dolly, a woman who by all accounts was as sweet as she was ancient, babysat them after school. She was in her late seventies, but spry, and never stopped moving the whole time she was in the house; cleaning, straightening, baking, folding, humming, helping. JJ went to work, came home, ate dinner, fell asleep in front of the TV. On weekends they all went to the girls' extracurriculars together; Lily had horse riding out at the Lakeland stables, and Emilia and Gracie had Irish dancing. JJ, to his credit, apparently attended both every week without fail. My father never even bothered to drop me off at a Cúl Camp. Their time was managed, predictable, with no room for spontaneity, which was how Máire liked things to be. The more she could control, the less chance of something terrible happening. She couldn't control me in the way she would have liked, so instead she

18

chastised me until I fell into step without really realising why. It only took her two goes at me for me to remember to turn the boiling kettle away from the cabinets, only one glare to shut the door after the dog. She took advantage of my fish-out-of-water position. I couldn't figure out where I fit in at all, so I just kind of floated around, pretending to get my bearings.

I was never mean to my sisters. I didn't want them to remember me as mean. I always humoured them, smiling at the way their faces developed a little blossom of pink when I listened with an interested expression to the babble that would stumble out of their mouths in their excitement to communicate their very important ideas to me. Lily had been wary at first, and for that, I felt sorry. The guilt gnawed at me when I thought of how coolly I'd disregarded her before I'd left, *bad sister* buzzing behind my eyes, neon and jarring. So I overcompensated, naturally. The Friday after my lamp got delivered, I was sitting at the breakfast table watching some vapid Instagram reel of a girl with overly tanned hands making a ridiculously decadent hot chocolate, melting a Hershey's bar into a mug of milk before stirring in a heaving glob of Nutella and topping it with a mountain of whipped cream and metallic sprinkles. The hot, dark liquid oozed over the side of the mug like sewage and I made a move to scroll on, sickened.

—Whoa.

I jumped at Lily's voice behind me, turning a *Jesus* into a *Janey* before it got the chance to leave my mouth.

—That looks lovely, doesn't it?

—If you can tell me one new thing you learned in school

today when you come back this evening, I'll make hot chocolates.

I had to go to town to meet Doireann and I hadn't asked for a lift yet. I was dreading it. I dumped the last of my tea into the sink and washed my mug quickly as my mother descended the stairs. I'd already turned her Keurig on in anticipation, placing her cup beneath the spout and popping the cappuccino pod into the top, leaving a Belvita breakfast biscuit next to it on the counter.

—Oh, aren't we feeling very thoughtful today?

—I know, I outdo myself.

I paused for a beat before forcing the words out of my mouth.

—Could I get a lift to town with you this morning?

She left me hanging for a good ten seconds before telling me to hurry up then, and I speed-walked to my room, drying my hands on the sleeves of my dressing gown, as she leaned back on the counter and left lipstick prints on the edge of her cup.

I had her drop me off at the top of the town, next to the statue of the two monks. The car was uncomfortably quiet once the girls got out at school, Lily holding Gracie's hand to walk her to the Infants classroom, Emilia with one knee-high sock already sinking down into her shoe. I envied them. I envied their lack of terrible knowledge. Even at Gracie's age, I had begun to understand the inevitability of suffering. My mother liked to say I had an *old soul*. I suspect it had more to do with the way we were living, just the two of us and occasionally my father, my mother having a perpetual emotional breakdown, me absorbing it all quietly, dutifully, like the walls of a padded cell. I stood in the shadow of the monks, smoking, surveying. The central stretch of the town was visible from here, beginning at Texas Department Store and ending on a leftward curve towards Main Street, cafés and boutiques and myriad faux-upscale shopfronts littering the sides of the road, all interchangeable, miraculous if they lasted a year each before closing and being replaced by something equally as ambitious. The paint might have changed but the shape of the town stayed ever the same underneath all that fuss; a snake full of elephants. I watched cars roll up and down the little bit of a hill and ran my tongue against the back of my teeth and let the rollie filter burn a blister to the inside of my lip on my last drag, using the pain to clear my head before taking off.

As I wandered in and out of everywhere, background details became jarring focal points. Euros on price tags. Lyons tea bags on the shelves of family-owned supermarkets named things like O'Meara's or Kenny's. The piddly town bus rounding, with a dangerous sidewards lean, the nipple of a roundabout outside McDonald's. Children in diesel-green and bottle-blue school uniforms with the names of saints stitched into the crests, smoking and flirting at the top of the canal walk. Every so often I'd see a face that looked too close to familiar and I'd find my exit route and return, again, to weaving the footpaths. I was breathless when I reached my destination; the café Doireann and I'd smoked fags behind when we'd mitched school on Fridays. It felt right for our reunion. I sat down outside and waited for her, knee jiggling under the table, hands pulled up into my sleeves. I would have ordered but I didn't know what Doireann liked anymore. I didn't know a lot of things anymore. There used to be a second-hand bookshop across from where I was sitting, the shelves sagging with paperbacks yellowed by the daylight, volumes and volumes of once-loved books that smelled like dusty vanilla, like old people's houses. Sometime in the last half a decade it had been replaced with a vape shop and I'd never even heard about it.

—Saoirse?

Doireann was blonde now. I knew that from her Instagram stories, but it was still a shock to see in person. She smiled and did this little high-pitched squeal and I did too, reflexively, before she hugged me harder than I'd ever been hugged in my life.

Doireann and I met on our first day of Junior Infants. We were sat next to each other because our surnames were neighbours in the alphabet. She had lopsided pigtails and a porridge stain on her pinafore, and when Miss Kearney handed out the modelling clay she mashed all the colours of hers together into one grey-brown lump before stretching it out the length of our shared desk and calling it Snakey. I liked her immediately. I was extremely quiet, small for my age, and my hair had never been cut; that morning my mother had clipped back the front with a series of butterfly-shaped plastic clasps and by the end of the day I'd gifted one to Doireann, which she snapped onto the strap of her backpack before our parents met us at the classroom door. Soon, we were inseparable. Everyone said our names like Thelma and Louise, like it felt wrong to them to say *Doireann* without *Saoirse* tacked on, like starting a sentence and abandoning it midway. When teachers wanted to punish one of us they'd make us sit separately; our Fifth Class teacher, in particular, took offence at our closeness, how we sometimes held hands and skipped during break or spent the time whispering among ourselves under the oil tank next to the boundary wall of the schoolyard, pulling up daisies and knotting them into crowns. She told our mothers that we were displaying *unhealthy boundaries* with one another, and for the rest of the school year, we were made to sit apart on either side of the classroom. We weren't allowed to pair off for projects or partner up on the school tour. It did not weaken our resolve. We made subtle moves to ensure we could pass each other on our way to and from the bathroom or stand together at the classroom bin and pare our pencils unnoticed. Too clever to chat and be heard, we'd slip lengthy notes into each other's hands. It was the closest I'd ever been to another human being. And then we went to separate secondary schools. She blossomed and I crept, but she never forgot about me, dragging me always into her light. She invited me to every birthday party, every sleepover. When her other friends confessed that they thought I was weird, or quiet, she would stand up for me, fierce and loyal to a fault. We went off to college together, me by the skin of my teeth, and were finally living our teenage dream, devised over the long afternoons where we'd both sneak out of our respective school grounds and meet up behind this café to split cigarettes stolen from my father's van. We both enrolled in an arts degree and shared a damp apartment in the shitty on-campus student accommodation. It was wonderful and exciting and fun and new and terrifying all the time. I got overwhelmed before we'd even had our Christmas exams. I couldn't keep up with the workloads, couldn't focus in lectures. I was drinking any night I could afford to, drinking to the point of blackout, and Doireann would have to get me home and remove my shoes and put me in the recovery position on my bed. And then one day, I went to my last class. And then I stopped going on nights out. And then I stopped going home at the weekends. And then I stopped leaving the apartment altogether. But I couldn't think about that now, or I'd turn heel and run before our coffees got to the table.

—*Céad míle fáilte*, bitch.

—I missed you.

—How was the trip home?

I told her about puking on the flight, about blocking James, about my sisters and about Máire, and she told me about her parents, and her job as a barista for a chain coffee place at the other end of town. She'd been working, saving to do her Higher Diploma in Galway, or maybe Dublin. I secretly thought she was mentally ill for wanting to teach geography. But she didn't go a bit mad and drop out in her first year, so what did I know?

—Any plans tonight?

—No.

—Ya do now. Get your sluttiest dress on, you're coming to a party and we're gonna pull you a fine thing.

—I don't want a fine thing. I don't want any thing.

—Well either way you're going.

—Who's party even is it?

—Some fella. The fella I'm seeing invited me.

My face must have fallen a mile.

—Pleaaaaase?

I wanted to say no, but unfortunately she had me at *sluttiest dress*; I'd already mentally planned an outfit. We agreed to meet at nine.

As soon as they came back from school Lily produced a recorder and played the first handful of notes of 'Little Donkey' three times, and was about to launch into a fourth rendition when I quickly clapped, bringing a swift and diplomatic end to the noise. That evening, as I pulled up the queasy Instagram reel once more to recreate the aesthetic of the hot chocolate that had enamoured Lily so, my mother hovered. She corrected – *don't put the cream in when it's too hot or it'll curdle; don't add more sugar, there's enough in the chocolate; Emilia doesn't like peppermint; Gracie can't have those sprinkles, they're a choking hazard.*

Despite my apparent inability to make a hot chocolate without parental supervision, the drinks were a hit. After the mugs had been drained, three wee girls were splayed across the comforter of my bed, cocoa-drunk, eyes trained on my laptop screen, Emilia dozing off, Gracie's mouth sticky at the corners with melted marshmallow. I was sitting cross-legged on the floor in front of a large mirror with an ornate frame made of sprayed plastic, pilfered off the wall in the hallway, carefully doing my makeup, hands slick from the nerves.

—That's pretty. Are you gonna do more glitter?

—What, you don't think it's too much?

I caught Lily's eye in the mirror and she shook her head.

—Needs more glitter like, up here.

She put a small hand to her eye and traced a curve under her brow bone. I mimicked the movement with a soft-domed

25

brush dipped in shimmering pigment, mapping nebulas beneath the dark barrier of my eyebrow. She grinned, her teeth all crooked, big, shiny new ones growing in next to baby ones still comfortable in their sockets for now, making me think of a child's skull sans flesh, and how the adult teeth nightmarishly sit in hollows above and below the gum line, waiting to emerge. I pushed the thought down before patting the floor next to me. She carefully climbed off the bed, Emilia and Gracie both asleep now. We sat cross-legged, facing one another, and I took her chin in my hand gently.

—Close your eyes.

I picked up the brush and softly, softly, pressed the loose glitter to her eyelids, swept some up her cheekbones, across the bow of her top lip.

—Now we match.

I left her sitting, gazing at herself, turning her head this way and that so her face would catch the light at different angles, and went to put my dress on.

I came down the stairs shoeless so I wouldn't break my neck, the heels dangling from my hand as I asked Máire for a taxi number.

—You look great. God be with the days when I had legs like that. Where are you going?

—I'm meeting Doireann.

—Doireann Moran?

—Yes, what other Doireanns do we know?

—I didn't know ye were still friends.

—Why wouldn't we be?

—There's no need to be so defensive, Saoirse, Jesus Christ, you're a constant briar.

26

Before I could cut her in two with a comment, JJ stood up from the sofa and shook his keys free from his jeans pocket. I swallowed the words like a dry pill.

—Save your money, I'll give you a lift.

The drive to the house party wasn't any longer than fifteen minutes, yet the silence made it feel like aeons. I hadn't anything to say to JJ really; the circles in our Venn diagram barely overlapped. But I couldn't bear an awkward silence. It made me feel edgy, worse again if I couldn't think of a single thing to say that might break it. Eventually JJ said:

—Your mother thinks the world of you, you know.

—I'll bet she does.

—She just worries. Ya haven't been too motivated.

—I've literally been back less than a fortnight. Am I not entitled to a bit of grace, no?

—It's about being an adult, Saoirse.

—When she was my age she was unemployed and left her kid with relatives so she could go on the piss for days at a time, so no, I don't think I'll be taking any life advice from her.

—Your mother had a hard life. I'm not trying to fight with you. Just… give some grace to get some back is all I'm saying. Always love your mother; you'll never get another.

I would have preferred the awkward silence. Shame burned my cheeks hot under the layers of makeup and I bit the inside of my mouth, hard, rolling the flesh between my back teeth. I leaned forward and turned on the radio. We listened wordlessly to 'The Patriot Game' by Liam Clancy the rest of the way. Perfect pre-party tune. I was fit to kill myself when we pulled up. I said thank you when I got out of the van; I was upset but I wasn't rude, and I really did appreciate the lift. Just not the scolding.

The door of the house was already ajar, people trickling onto the lawn and into the footpath. I made a beeline for the living room where I found Doireann on the sofa, looking so divine that I felt myself shrink at the sight of her. She hovered up from the cushions and threw her arms across my shoulders, pulling me into her, the smell of hairspray and false tan sticking itself to my denim jacket. I accepted the hug haphazardly, feeling my dress lift from my thighs as I stretched over. The coffee table was littered with alcohol, Aldi white wine and Orchard Thieves and 70cl bottles of Smirnoff. I kept my drink in my bag, too paranoid of being spiked and making a show of myself. She turned back to a boy I hadn't seen sitting next to her, GAA jersey with the sleeves rolled up, unmistakably Irish red hair mussed and gelled, skinny legs stretched out in front of him blocking the way out of the room while he scrolled on his phone, idle.

—We'll be back. Sersh, grab two cans there and let's go have a fag.

She led the way through the busy kitchen. Music that made my ears itch poured from a tall speaker in the corner and I tried not to look anyone in the face, afraid someone would recognise me and I'd have to pretend to care about seeing them. I just didn't have that level of commitment to the bit when I was sober. We made it through without being stopped, down to the rockery, hidden from the back door, the motion-sensor lamp dancing on the sequins of Doireann's slip dress on our way past. I had a can of lukewarm cider tucked under each arm, walking on the balls of my feet to stop my heels from sinking into the lawn, my toes stretching and aching with the effort.

I was a woman who had issues with other women. Inherited, I was fairly sure, from my mother, and her from her own mother, and so on. Intergenerational awkwardness, passed down like mother of pearl earrings or a lace wedding veil, from one pale, spindly hand to another. Neither Máire nor Granny Lynch had a single close female friend that wasn't a blood relative; nobody to drink wine and do brunch with, nobody to power-walk the roads with, nobody to ring up and bitch to for an hour while they folded the clothes or made the bed. I was no different in my burgeoning adult-hood. Outside of Doireann, I'd never learned how to bond with another girl on that labyrinthine, complicated level that other women seem to form their friendships. I'd never had a big group of girlfriends, never been a bridesmaid, a godmother, not even a 3 a.m. emergency-call contact. I eventually had friends in secondary school, but I was so nervous about seeming abnormal to them that I put myself in increasingly dangerous and uncomfortable situations just to project an image of myself that was, to me and to them, socially acceptable. This was not the kind of friend group that would, say, encourage you to wear an ugly fedora just because you like it, or the kind of friend group that would give you a hug when you show up to school crying because your parents are getting a divorce. No, this was the other kind of friend group; the one that gives you your first drink, your first fag, sets up your first tongue kiss at a teenage disco. The kind that giggles behind their hands when you show up to school with a wonky fringe or a new set of braces. The kind that, you know on some level, will be your friends for precisely as long as it takes for you all to graduate, before they disappear into the ether, confined in your adult years purely to Facebook updates and chance encounters in supermarkets.

Doireann, on the other hand, made friends with everyone. She was the nexus being of all her social circles; people who would normally never deign to speak to one another suddenly found themselves sitting together chatting like they gave a shit about what the other had to say, purely because they were all gathered there for the love of Doireann. At Christmas, when everyone returned from their far-flung corners of the earth, her Instagram was flooded with ten-slide posts of her cliques, groups of girls wearing jewel-toned satin dresses and strappy heels all bent uncomfortably at the knee, stoners and skaters from her emo phase gathered in a smoking area with her in the middle beaming, her gaggle of cousins hovering around a Christmas tree in her granny's house. Despite never being invited, I flipped through the photos intently every time they cropped up on my feed, and clicked around the name tags until I had a stomach ache.

She stuck a flame to the end of a cigarette and I perched on a flat, hard edge of the rockery, the skeletal leaves of a fern grazing my elbows. It smelled like home – mulch and weeds and cut grass and damp air, always saturated, pregnant with rain.

—So.

—So.

I took the cigarette from her long fingers and punctuated with a lengthy exhale through the nostrils, eyes closed.

—You look like you needed that.

—You've no idea.

—Don't be greedy. Starved for a bit of gossip.

I didn't want to talk about Máire, so I told her about James instead.

—I stalked his socials earlier. It hasn't been a month and he's seeing someone.

It was true. I couldn't help myself. I looked at those photos knowing they'd make me blind, knowing they'd burn themselves into the back of my head. His friends and family commented things like *gorgeous couple!!* and *you look so happy mate* and *congrats luv xx*, all people I'd either never met or who didn't like me. That was the salt in the wound.

—The dirty bastard. Who is she? Do you know her?

—No. Some yoke. Bottle blonde. Probably Tinder.

—What's her name?

She pulled out her phone and searched her on Facebook.

—Fucking hell. Common as muck. Eyebrows like brackets. He was punching with you anyway.

That made me feel a bit better. I'd pored over his new girlfriend's profile with the keen, searching eye of a forensic analyst, and all I'd gotten back was confirmation of my own inferiority. She'd gotten a Facebook Official hard-launch in less than one month from a man who hadn't so much as introduced me to his parents in nearly three years. That surely meant that I was worth less than her in some way, or many ways. *Studied at Queen's University Belfast. Works at Great Ormond Street Children's Hospital. Checked in at Virgin Active Gym. In a relationship with James Harris.* I looked back to the house for a moment, the windows ameliorating blades of grass and shrubbery with a warm, ochre light. The garden was painfully average, a patch of grass and concrete surrounded by splintering wood panelling. Someone had tried to make it pretty once, but the flowers had died and the rockery was just a hole with bark chips in it now, three languid plants sprawling across the edges, their roots strangled by dandelions and crabgrass. I closed my eyes and emptied my mind of everything I hated. I thought of sunshine, of glittering waves at the edge of the earth, of the indiscernible line where the sky meets the sea, dotted with boats and tanned backs and parasols perfectly still in the thick heat. Then I washed it all away with a mouthful of Bulmers.

—Whose gaff is this again?

—See him on the right side of the kitchen window?

A boy our age stood with one hand on the back of his prematurely balding head, the other holding a can of something I couldn't make out from my distance, a white football jersey of some sort riding up to reveal a little strip of hairy belly. He was forty-five at twenty-two. I would have bet my life he smelled like Lynx body spray and fried sausages. He was below me in school – I recognised, under a scrape of stubble, the soft, edgeless curve of his jaw, the top teeth that overlapped like the dog-eared pages of a book. Small towns breed that level of perception.

—What do you think of him?

—Um. Not my type?

She was quiet for a split second before bursting into laughter, and I joined in, and it felt good to be in sync with someone, and strange that we'd fallen back into step with one another so quickly. Before we got up to go back in, she told me she was glad I came. Then she stuck a hand down her dress and into the left cup of her bra, rooting around for something, sticking her tongue out in concentration.

—Well I'm running low on inspirational quotes and stellar life advice, but can I interest you in a commiseratory trip instead?

She lightly shook a small, crumpled baggie in my direction. Inside, little green tabs of acid hopped around the corners as she waved it at me. I was surprised. I'd never seen Doireann abuse substances before. I was the one who was supposed to do that. I got over the shock quickly though, and *only half* had flown from my throat with a split second of hesitation. Not my first rodeo. I bared my tongue, soft and pink, and Doireann split the tab with a thumbnail before placing half on the broad of it. She took the other half, and together we turned back towards the house arm in arm, giggling, footfalls jittery, excitement skittering from my belly to my legs. I forgot about my shoes and began sinking backwards precariously, trapped in the soft dirt by four inches of stiletto. Instead of fighting it I slipped my feet from the straps and left the shoes there; they weren't going anywhere.

Back on the sofa, I was nervous; my eyes couldn't settle on any one thing for too long and I was careful to avoid people's faces. I didn't want a stranger to think I was staring at them, paranoid of an argument, of rubbing someone up the wrong way. I was always like this during the half-hour after ingesting a substance. I hated waiting for whatever it was to kick in, remorse swirling in my unsettled stomach, almost not wanting to be high anymore before it even happened. Acid was the worst; already a nausea-heavy buzz, my anxiety made it worse and worse and generally I ended up being sick before I could settle into the trip properly. The first time I tripped was in the apartment with James and Helen. I took the tab, swallowed and immediately began to freak out. Helen laughed and James tried to make me do deep breathing while I just said *I don't want to be high anymore* over and over before puking into our mixing bowl; then I was fine. It changed my life. It was like somebody splayed out all the tangled cables of my brain, labelled and colour-coded them. On the comedown, I lay on James's chest crying silently because I could finally see that the world was so beautiful and that I was lucky to be alive in it. I was back to normal by the next weekend.

Doireann introduced me to Connor. He eyed me and said *well*, low and bored, before picking up his phone again.

—He can't get any white so he's pissy. Never mind him.

—Have ye been seeing each other long?

—It's…newish. We'll see how it goes. Christ.

She started to giggle and her pupils were dilating, getting bigger and bigger, swallowing all the light. I excused myself to find a bathroom, and moved like a vibrating fluid through the hallway, pouring myself into each step, holding onto the banister of the stairs as I tried to ascend them. Someone kindly pointed me to the left and I made it to the toilet bowl just in time. As predicted, once I puked I felt great. I rinsed my mouth with some Listerine I found on the windowsill and looked in the mirror above the sink, the last time I could look into a mirror all evening. Lily was right; the glitter beneath my brow bone set my eyes on fire, gas-flame blue and blazing. A hazy smile split my lips, teeth curling, dog-like.

—That kicking in?

Back on the sofa with no idea how I got there. Doireann looked as spacey as I felt. Connor was gone. I nodded and sat back, pulling my legs up so a stranger could pass me, tucking my bare feet in under my legs. The stranger sat next to me instead, occupying space I hadn't even noticed. The weight of his flesh sank the couch cushions and my innards sloshed a little, the hair on my arms bristling.

—Well.

—Well. Where were you?

Doireann eyed him before passing him a can.

—Wouldn't you like to know.

—Charlie, Saoirse. Saoirse, Charlie. Connor's BFFF.

—What's the extra F for?

—Best Fucking Friend Forever, obviously.

And she started to giggle again. I stuck out my hand to him and he grasped it gently, rough, warm fingers enveloping mine like a rosebud closing. The heat buried itself into my veins and ran up my arm, making me shiver. I met his eyes and felt a pull deep in my belly. They were impossibly green and crinkled at the corners when he spoke, framed in dark, thick lashes like the bare branches of a chestnut tree, topping a straight nose and a pronounced cupid's bow, off-setting a strong jaw, angular, masculine, marred with auburn stubble. It was art in that moment, kaleidoscopic, and I stared until his lines began to blur, the colours melding together, becoming abstract, an impression of something heavenly.

—Eh…is she alright?

—Never mind her, she's coming up.

—Jasus. Any left?

Soon we were all sitting like pigeons on the perch of the couch, staring at the fire, at each other, at ourselves. The world became a complicated mosaic that switched around and melted, stitching itself back together in the corner of my eye and falling apart again when I focused on it. Hours passed like honey oozing from a dipper. Somebody put YouTube on the TV, nominated themselves as living room DJ, switched from Yves Tumor to MGMT to Tame Impala to Mac DeMarco, and every track seemed to sync up perfectly with the swell and ebb of hallucination. I watched the walls breathe, deep in the chest of some great being, swelling and shrinking to fit a narrative my brain could not comprehend. We were all made of stardust; loose atoms and glittering molecules, glued together by the idea of meaning something. Mattering. Matter was the only matter and my eyes could not make it stick. In my third eye I could see the earth, a round blue ball hovering on the edge of nothingness, swathed in cloud and swirled with moss. I was not visible. I was not even a speck, a wink, a sparkle. I was nothing, just as everyone around me was nothing, bacteria on the crag of a rock hurtling through a vacuum with no understanding of the beginning or the end, or what comes after the end, or if anything even came before the beginning or after the end. Everything I had done and ever would do amounted to a flatline this far up. In the glaring darkness of the Milky Way, my emotions were moot, my experiences a blip on an infinite calendar, a dot of ink on the trillionth Friday of the billionth April of the millionth year. *I am a void*, I whispered to myself, peeling apart my teeth to let out a low, long breath. I was clammy; I did not notice until my dress began to stick to the skin between my shoulder blades. Heat crept up my neck and into my face, another wave of elation breaking across the skin of my cheeks, my chest, rippling to my fingertips and pooling in my stomach. I had to swallow the nausea. I couldn't even think of my can of cider.

—Ya alright?

Charlie's voice was like birdsong through water. We'd stayed in each other's orbit all night. I smiled lazily, nodded, took the joint he was holding and put it to my mouth. It felt like nothing pressed between my lips. He grinned back, Cheshire-wide and pearlescent, the corners of his mouth reaching up to meet his earlobes. My legs were draped over his and our forearms were touching and I thought about kissing him but didn't know if I could focus long enough.

Long after midnight, Connor showed up again, much livelier now, and the cokeheads piled into the living room, lines done out on dinner plates, rolled-up twenties at the ready. A girl I didn't know sat on the arm of the sofa next to me and a sheaf of her long, straightened, dark hair fell across my shoulder. The smell of her shampoo was the same as my mother's and I could instantly feel the anxiety building up inside me, the panic breaking out across me. I tried to clear my throat and started to cough and then I couldn't get in enough oxygen and my downward spiral started, my *I don't want to be high anymore* chant was internal and incessant, way too late in the game to do anything about it, and when I went to stand up I knocked almost every single bottle off the coffee table with my knees and people started to yell at me, admonishing, and Doireann just looked on wide-eyed. I stood, barefoot, jelly-legged, frozen, no breath in my lungs,

not able to see straight, a sense of impending doom drap-
ing itself around my shoulders like a yoke. Then, *it's only
the drugs* murmured in my ear, a firm hand on my elbow,
guiding me out through the kitchen and back to the garden,
sitting me down on the damp grass. Charlie. Even in the
dark, his eyes were visible, the whites snow-white, the green
irises plutonium-rich and glowing.

—Lie back.

—What?

—Lie back on the grass, like this.

He lay down. After a wary second, I did too.

—Take in a breath, I haven't heard you breathe in an age.

—I am breathing.

—A big breath, ya ejit.

So I took a big breath. And then another, and another, and
with every big breath the yoke got looser and looser until it
fell away, and I was saved, saved from the brink of a bad trip,
from the kind of mental wobble it could take weeks, possibly
even months, to recover from. Charlie breathed with me,
big, steady gusts in and out, a bellow of air scooped from
the ether and returned each time. It was maybe half an hour
before the sun would start to turn the sky from black to blue
and the stars were still visible.

—There's the Plough.

Charlie lifted his hand and traced the seven stars. I followed his finger with reverence, trying to make the pinpricks
of light stay in their fixed spots.

—And Orion.

This time he lifted my hand and conjured a hunter,
bow poised, belt buckled, stance steady. The feel of his

skin against mine was shocking, hot after the frigidity of the grass. I was over the peak of my high, I noticed; the butterflies he gave me felt closer to earth than anything else. As he waved my index finger around the sky like a sparkler, I turned my face towards his. He was unfairly good-looking, even with the angles of his bones so unsteady under my gaze.

—What?

—You saved me. Back there, I mean.

—Not at all. Connor's a mate but the vibe was fucked the second the cartel rolled in. I wanted out anyway.

—Very aggressive bunch, aren't they?

—Pack of coked-up wankers. Not that there's anything wrong with coke. Just wankers. The coke didn't ask to be up the nose of a wanker, did it?

—I suppose not.

—Smoke?

—A fag?

—I've a joint in my pocket either.

I said yes to the joint. We stayed lying down, passing it back and forth, watching all the constellations disappear into deepest morning blue.

—Walk you home?

—We'd be walking a fair while. I live out the far side of town.

—Walk you to the taxi rank then?

I dug my shoes out of the lawn and strapped them back onto my feet, my bare soles dirty and cold now, grass stains colouring the skin on the edge of my heel. He grabbed my hand and held it all the way. He kissed the back of it when he let it go again, said *I'll see you later, trouble.* He grinned at me as my taxi pulled away, the dawn illuminating him, the light attracted to him.

I was smitten. I was doomed.

II

—*Shh.*

—Mammy said to wake her.

—I *know* what Mammy said, Gracie.

I rolled over and opened my eyes. Emilia and Gracie stood clad in matching school uniforms at the end of the bed.

—Mammy said to wake you up. We brought you tea, it's on the locker.

—Go on. I'll be down in a bit.

Emilia grabbed Gracie's hand then and tugged her towards the door. When they were gone I sat up, brought the steaming cup to my lips and sighed with the effort of being alive. I'd stayed up late on the phone to Charlie for the third night in a row. At the time it seemed like a good idea; I had no reason that I knew of to be up before midday. Apparently, my mother did not agree. I felt hungover, lips slightly swollen, hair matted, and cold sweat drying into the oversized, faded blue t-shirt I had rooted out of one of my boxes from the attic the night before. It had the words *Carolina Tar Heels* on the front, the graphic stretched and cracked from washes, a well-meant gift from visiting American cousins.

I wondered how it survived Máire's purge when my debs dress hadn't even made the cut. She was probably still worried about offending them. What if they visited again and asked about the shirt? She'd die of the mortification.

My stomach had sunk at my sisters' liberal use of the name *Mammy*, a name I was not, under any circumstances, allowed to use for my mother. No Mammys, Mummys, Mams, Mums, Mas or Auld Ones had been permitted to pass my lips since I'd said my first word – which was, funnily enough, *Kieran*, my father's name. Máire had been devoted to her mission of remaining young, cool and definitely not someone's mother. So I'd been exclusively calling her Máire since the age of about three. In Junior Infants, when other kids picked up on this idiosyncrasy, I'd been mildly bullied. I tried to get away with calling my mother Mammy when I got home that afternoon and received the most serious bollocking of my young life thus far. Her voice was even and deadly, and almost two decades on, it rang in my head clear as a bell.

—I was christened Máire Lynch. Not Mammy. That is not my name. I won't speak to you if you don't use my name. Do you understand?

I had nodded, hand to my mouth most likely, chewing on the whittles of my fingertips – a habit that formed when I grew too old for the dummy and one I was still prone to. I never called her anything but her own name ever again. But here we were, twenty-odd years on, and her new family were happily bleating pet names to one another over and over, like we were in an episode of *7th Heaven*. I was pathetically sour about it. Jealous of three little kids. It was sad of me, really.

—Up! Up!

Máire burst into the room and threw back the curtains before flinging the window open.

—Jesus, Saoirse, you look like a vagrant. Take a shower, you've a job interview at twelve.

—I didn't get any call for an interview.

Endless hours spent editing and distributing a CV that listed my greatest achievement as winning Bronze in the An Gaisce award had amounted to three rejections and radio silence.

—I know. Do you remember Paul and Rosie McLaughlin? McLaughlin's? The hardware shop on the Dublin road? Rosie is JJ's cousin.

Everyone was a cousin of everyone in the hellscape of my hometown. Here, she paused momentarily to check herself in the small round mirror hanging above the chest of drawers, running her ring fingers under her eyes to catch stray eyeshadow.

—He's arranged for you to go in and have a chat. I picked you out one of my blouses, it shouldn't be too small, but if it is I'm sure there's something else. Come on, up.

She tried to tug at the duvet and I gripped it tightly to my chin.

—Jesus, Máire, I've no bottoms on. I'm getting up, alright? Just give me a minute.

—Saoirse, it's a quarter past eight on a Thursday. I'm just saying.

She left then, a flurry of musky, expensive scents and carefully blow-dried hair. I sat up fully and watched from the window as the girls plodded out behind her in their

43

matching French plaits, burgundy cardigans, shiny patent shoes, and grey pinafores. Lily looked the most like me; we both had the same shade of neutral brown hair, our mother's natural colour, blonde as babies, ageing into brunette. In extended exposure to daylight, the colour took on buttery highlights. I could see the strands brightening now in the morning sun. Emilia and Gracie, dark and curly-headed like JJ, took their cues from Lily; they fell into step behind her so naturally, always aware of her movements, and of the disapproving look she would give them if they deviated from her expectations. She was the eldest sister, after all. A certain responsibility came with that.

When Máire told me she was pregnant with Lily, I felt indifferent. She'd gone to the trouble of getting me a card that said something like *To The Best Big Sister*, a picture of her twelve-week scan tucked inside of it. I stared at the little blob on the stiff square of paper and forced a big smile and hugged her and said I was delighted. But I already knew. Hill Lodge was so small that I'd heard her discussing names with JJ at night. Máire said she wanted to name her something beautiful, something delicate. They were married by then, and already, before she'd even handed me the card, she had been pulling away from me. Gone was the need for me, the dependence on me as her only source of reassurance. She made me the keeper of her happiness and then blithely unmade me, like it was nothing. JJ was her knight in shining tinfoil, and I was demoted to teenage headache. She had Lily, and I stayed with Granny Lynch for a week while she *adjusted* to being at home with a newborn. When I was allowed to come back, I kept my distance. I watched my mother fall in love with Lily from the far side of the sofa, only a faint kind of jealousy rousing within me as she cooed and kissed and melted when Lily wrapped her stumpy fist around her pinky finger. Before her first birthday, my mother was pregnant again, and JJ's distaste for Hill Lodge became harder and harder for Máire to side-step. He didn't like the damp. He didn't think the bathroom was big enough. He didn't think it was fair that Lily and the new baby would have to share a room. He didn't think the garden was secure enough for Max, his big, soft ejit of a gun dog. I felt the end of something coming nearer and nearer and I couldn't bear to sit around waiting for it. I started to spend my evenings with the bad kind of friends, only coming home at night like an outdoor cat, feeding and sleeping before leaving again, and each time I returned I felt the space for me in the house grow tighter. That's when Máire and I started fighting. She'd catch me sneaking back in my bedroom window drunk and stoned at 3 a.m., or I'd go missing from Friday to Sunday and she'd cry and roar at me and take my phone and give it back a day later after having thoroughly searched it, no wiser, no better off. She said she didn't know what to do with me. Neither did I.

In Lily's toddlerhood, despite her best efforts to charm me, I remained unmoved. On the rare occasions I'd be obliged to spend time in the house, she would seek me out with the incorrigible curiosity of a cat that's spotted a shrew in the long grass. She'd offer me her apple slices smeared in peanut butter, wave books at me in the hopes I'd read them to her, and insist on showing me all of her individual toys, one by one. I humoured it as a babysitter might, but I wasn't devastated to leave her behind, even though she clung to my hand at the airport. Emilia, too young at the time to understand, was quacking indiscriminately from inside her pram, one sock missing and the other precariously dangling from her toes, and Gracie had yet to drop. Máire shed a few tears, although I suspected that had more to do with being heavily pregnant in a muggy airport than it did with my emigration. She did hug me though, long and tight, longer than necessary, her tears leaving the shoulder of my jumper damp. I was crying too, even though I fought it harder than I'd fought anything in my stubborn life. It was a relief, in the end, to step onto the plane.

Remembering the day I emigrated gave me a sudden shock of guilt. I sat on the edge of the bed, bottomless, bare feet cold on the floor, legs prickly and unshaven, the light making the blonde hair glow. My attic boxes, all three of them, lay open next to me, the contents briefly skimmed before I went to bed. I'd gone up and taken them down myself, scurrying across exposed roof beams with my phone torch on, wrangling the cardboard cubes down the bandy attic ladder one by one. Everything inside of them smelled of must. Content highlights included my Communion dress, my set of Harry Potter books with the fifth one missing, my handwriting copy from Junior Infants, three cheap gold ban-gles from Penneys, my Leaving Cert hoodie, a small stack of CDs, two sets of jeans that definitely did not fit me anymore, a framed photo of Doireann and me when we were about ten, and the t-shirt I was currently wearing. I ran an index finger over my crooked little letters etched so painstakingly into the wide lines of the copy pages, *a e i o u* written over and over again until the pencil strokes started to look a little more light-handed, a little less effortful. Before I got dressed, I rooted out the photo of Doireann and me again, snapped a picture of it with my phone and sent it to her. I aimed a gentle kick at the boxes, nudging them under the bed where I couldn't see them anymore. Then I wiped the sleep from my eyes, pulled on my dressing gown and went for a shower.

I did my best thinking in the bath and my worst in the shower. That day was no exception. Before the water was even hot on my back I had settled into a mental strut of questions with no good answers. Dear God, why couldn't Máire just leave me alone? Why couldn't she let me find my own fecking job in my own time? Why did she have to infiltrate every corner of my life with her suggestions and her comments and her expectations and her disappointment? Why did I even come back here in the first place? Why did James have to dump me? Why was I so difficult to love? Why did I move in with him in the first place, why did I even say hello to him that first night, why did I leave my first houseshare, why did I bother emigrating, why did Granny Maher have to die, why didn't I stay in college or even do a course, why didn't I have a single iota of ambition? Why didn't I care enough about anything to be anything worth caring about? All of this by the end of my second shampoo cycle; strands of hair came loose around my fingers as I scrubbed furiously at my scalp as if I could lather and rinse my brain and step out of the shower stall a new person, freshly sluiced clean of all previous terrible ideas. No such luck, but the vigorous wash did my hair the world of good and that improved my mood slightly.

I hadn't even considered the actual mechanics of the job interview until I was sitting in the passenger seat of my mother's car. She, of course, drove me to the interview. She was using a day of her annual leave to do this. She informed me of this like it was a favour I'd owe back. She plugged the aux cord into her phone and put on an Enrique Iglesias mix, the volume on two, like music in a doctor's waiting room. The car was big, slick, the seats a fresh cream colour; I wondered how she kept it clean with the girls still so young, sticky-handed and mucky. I would have destroyed them the day the car was brought home simply by existing. In fact, sitting there at my big age of twenty-three, I was pretty certain I'd end up leaving a smudge on something before we reached our destination. I decided to lean into it.

—Can I smoke a rollie with the window down, please?

—Roll it all the way down or JJ will think I'm at them again. Not that he can talk.

She licked her lips when I pressed the flame to the end.

—Do you miss them?

—Every now and again. You should quit.

—I know. I will. When I'm no longer in my early twenties and immune to death.

She laughed but it was a weird sound. The fairies had left me a changeling.

—Same old smart-arse.

She took her eyes off the road to glance at me. She had new wrinkles around the sockets; little rivulets, cracks in the plaster bust. I marvelled at them internally.

—Keeps it interesting, doesn't it?

—I suppose. JJ thinks you've an acid tongue. Keep it in check around the girls, I don't want them picking up your bad habits.

—And where does he think I got my smart mouth from, licked it off the ground?

—Very good.

—Poor JJ. Blessed is he amongst women.

—Poor nothing.

She indicated for the industrial estate too late and the car behind slapped on the brakes with a screech. The seatbelt bit into the skin of my collarbone.

—Prick!

She violently and repeatedly stabbed the hazard light button with two fingers while beeping the horn.

—Would ye go again for a boy or does he mind?

—Oh God no; three kids is enough for me, I couldn't go again.

She put her hand on the back of my seat to reverse, her neck craned, sun-spotted from tanning beds.

—Four.

—What?

She was distracted, the car almost too big for the parking space.

—You have four kids.

—Oh yeah. You know what I mean. Can I've the end of that?

She gestured to the rollie, down to the last few pulls. I handed it to her before clicking open my belt.

—Don't be nervous. Tell them you know JJ; you'll be flying.

I nodded and began to disembark from the car carefully; we were so close to the van beside us I had to get out one limb at a time, opening the door until it gently touched off the side, hands and feet mindfully unfolding like a contortionist exiting a suitcase.

—Watch my door.

She was savouring the yellowed butt of my cigarette, inhaling the smoke like it was the rich aroma of the finest cigar, letting it sit in her lungs before reluctantly releasing it to the ether.

—I'll be here. Don't take ages, I've stuff to do.

—I can't control how long the interview is going to be.

—Yeah well, just don't dawdle.

I freed my right ankle and snapped the door shut, resisting the urge to grab her wing mirror and pull it clean off, my fingers aching with the want. I didn't look back, instead keeping my eyes low the whole way to the automatic doors of the shop, stepping on cracks in the tarmac on purpose.

The hardware shop was bigger than it looked from the outside; it sank into the ground, several steps down, before sprawling towards the back where a little garden centre stood, plants leaning and sagging in a climate too wet for them. It was busy for a Thursday morning, or busier than I expected. I stood at the deserted customer service counter as tired, middle-aged people shuffled between aisles carrying buckets of white ceiling paint or sets of Allen keys or a new yard brush, symbols of mundanity, of obligatory upkeep. I was twelve minutes early. Thoughts of sabotage were floated; I could just potter around the garden centre for twenty minutes and tell Máire I didn't get the job. I could pick my nose during the interview. I could just tell them to fuck off either. Knowing I was only ever a well-uttered *fuck off* away from exile was comforting. My phone vibrated inside the front pocket of my handbag. A text from Charlie.

You busy tonight?

A woman, short, wiry, and hard-faced, began to approach me, and I had to leave him hanging.

—Can I help you?

—Hi, I've an interview?

I said it like a question and her mouth turned down at the corners. I knew she could already smell my weaknesses.

—Follow me.

She led me to a small, pokey office to the right of the shop, through a rickety plywood door marked *PRIVATE*. The office consisted of one desk with a dining chair on either side, mismatched, one with a curved back and the other straight. I watched as she sidled around the desk, back almost pressed against an industrial shelf bursting with rag-gedy notebooks, shoeboxes, and loose leaves of paper. I sat in the chair facing her, my handbag on my lap.

—You can get comfortable. I don't bite. Rosie. Saoirse?

I nodded and she stuck out a hand, the back of which was ageing and rough. I grasped it and noticed my palm was slick. When I took mine back, I put my bag on the ground and dragged my fingers across the rough denim of my jeans. My mother's blouse, predictably, hadn't fit me; my chest was bigger than hers and it strained against the seersucker. I had dug out a black jumper from my suitcase and quickly ironed out the travel creases. Maybe I imagined it, already wounded by the evident failure of my body to take up as little room as possible, but Máire looked a bit satisfied when I told her the blouse hadn't gone past my bra.

—So you're Máire's prodigal daughter. I have to say, you don't take after her at all.

—No, everyone says I look more like my father.

She was taking stock of me now, eyeing me, beady and razor-precise. I wondered what she made of me. Probably not much. She could probably see the Maher shape of my face, the natural defiance of my brow. I sat up straighter.

—Right, brass tacks, my dear, because I don't have all day. Why do you want to work here?

My response was measured but honest.

—Because I need the money. And the sales experience.

—Fair. See a lot of bar work on here but no shop work. Do you know how to use a till?

I nodded.

—And you've obviously dealt with the general public, yes?

I nodded again. The less I said the more pleased she seemed.

—Okay. So the hours are part time, Monday, Wednesday and alternating weekends. Usually a full-day shift so nine to six. Thirteen euro an hour. That sound agreeable?

One more nod. She returned it this time. I decided I liked her already.

—Right. So can we say I'll see you on Monday week bright and early?

—Do I need to bring anything?

I had seen other staff in a loose sort of uniform; a polo shirt with the *McLaughlin's Hardware* logo stitched to the right breast, and black trousers.

—Just yourself, black trousers, and shoes. We'll give you a polo shirt when you get here. The floor manager is Nadia, you'll meet her on Monday and she'll go over the rest of the ins and outs with you. Tell your parents I said hello.

I thanked her and left. I skipped the crack-stepping on the way back to my mother's car and texted Charlie back, giddy, hands shaking.

Not yet. Why?

———

That night, they picked me up at the end of the boreen, far enough away from my mother's house that I wouldn't have to tell her who it was. The cherry-red brake lights loomed out of the dark, the soft gold glow of the back-seat light haloing three heads and six shoulders. Doireann was already in the passenger seat, her hair and face done in a way that said *low-maintenance* but that I knew had taken her a while; individual lashes, freshly dyed brows, a soft wave curled into her ends. I, by comparison, had tried to wing my eyeliner and ended up crying in frustration at my inability to make the shapes match. I gave up, scrubbed at my eyes with a baby wipe and rushed through two coats of mascara instead. I was quietly furious at myself for being so useless, and at Doireann for being so pretty. Charlie was in the back and Connor was driving, which made me nervous, but I pushed it down. I got in, folded myself to fit into the narrow space behind Doireann's seat, tried not to jostle Charlie's hands as they flipped a joint in his lap. He looked at me before he reached up and flicked off the light. I wanted his fingers knotted in my hair. I wanted to kiss every knuckle delicately.

—Well.

A chorus of *wells* was returned, and as Charlie stuck a Bic to the end of the joint the car pulled away from the verge and snaked off down the unmarked, hardly tarred road.

—Open that back window, can't have the stink of hash if we get pulled over.

I cranked the handle until the air was blustering, turning my cheeks sticky-cool, the night bathing them. Charlie called *tick* and my *tock* was the first out. He passed me the smoke and I tried to look alluring as I pressed it to my lips, blowing out in a long, smooth stream, my breath lost to the ditches. I was quietly obsessed with him; my nights out had become discreet safaris, eyes peeled for the sight of him at the bar or in the smoking area, and after a drunken fumble or three we started texting, and then one night he rang me, smoke heavy in his voice, my gut fluttering at the deep, scratchy, satisfying sound of it. We'd stay on the phone until one of us was nodding off, neither wanting to hang up first, and then one would say goodnight reluctantly, sleep too tempting to fight anymore. When I wasn't speaking to him, I was thinking about him, though I'd been trying to stay a little aloof; he hadn't asked me on anything close to a date yet. But he and Connor did ask Doireann and me to come out in the car this evening, and both she and I agreed that was *kind of* a double date.

The act of driving with no destination was one of the few sanctioned freedoms in the town. Boys got their licence at seventeen, not to be able to drive themselves to school or run errands for their mothers, but to cruise the back roads at elevated speeds with the stereo rattling the windows. Maybe they'd drive a girl to a ghost estate or the lakeshore and get a clumsy blowjob in the driver's seat. Maybe they'd idle all the way to the next town over at two in the morning for no other reason than the opportunity to see a different set of place names on the road signs. This was the allowance the community made for providing so little else in the way of autonomy; soon they would have to get jobs in supermarkets, construction sites, bars, garages, and factories, and not long after that middle age would knock. For the most part, there would be no universities, European city breaks, or general adventure. Maybe not even a house, because there were fuck all left to buy and even less to rent. Emigration was a popular parachute, but many hadn't the means to get an Australian visa in the first place, bank accounts with nothing in them but the price of an expensive coffee. On the precipice of adulthood, these truths could lead to death if acknowledged too sharply. Everyone knew someone who couldn't hack it, was someone who couldn't hack it, not suited to the threat of a mediocre life, someone who had jumped into the canal or fallen backwards onto the train tracks or swallowed a whole handful of yokes with a vodka chaser, leaving the rest of us to fill the ever-yawning jagged maw of the town with our sadness and our children's sadness and our children's children's sadness, one big soul-sucking plughole of a town, nothing left in the end but the dregs of well-known families and local alcoholics. But as long as there were wheels to move cars, the roads would offer up the suggestion of an indeterminate destiny.

I was delighted to find that, for the second time that day, I felt pleasant; it had been so long since I'd felt anything but tired. This part of me was cobwebby, dusty; it rattled alive now, gears oiled with THC and petrol fumes. We sped past my primary school, closed now, the dropping numbers of country children a key factor in the unceremonious chaining of the gates and boarding of the windows.

—I went there.

This indisputable fact anchored me, in my mind, to this place, and to the people in this place, earned me my spot in this back seat, proved my good country stock and dismissed the slightly British twang I had picked up during my time away.

—So did I. How did your job thing go today?

Doireann burst my stoney nostalgia bubble with her question. I pulled my face back in the window and wound it up a little.

—Oh grand. Got the job. Start next week.

Everyone congratulated me and it was genuine. Shovelling shit, serving pints, cleaning toilets, assembling car parts – it didn't matter what the job was, as long as it was yours you'd get the same pat on the back as if you'd just become a paediatric surgeon or a rocket scientist. Charlie found my leg in the dark, pressed his lips to my ear when nobody was paying attention, his voice a throaty hum inside my skull. My pulse flowed freely, climbing at the vibration of the door speakers, buzzing in my chest at the claim he laid to me. My face turned pink with pleasure. He made me glow in the dark.

When we'd run out of routes to drive, they dropped me back off at the end of Máire's road. I got out reluctantly, a little afraid to walk back up to the house alone, very stoned and with no battery left in my phone to run the flashlight.

—Sure I'll walk you up the road. Con, will ya circle back for me?

Connor nodded and Charlie got out after me. The butterflies in my gut were violent. I stopped at the passenger window to say goodbye to Doireann, who widened her eyes at me and glanced back at Charlie as if to say *go get your man*. They drove off and then it was just us two, enveloped in the dark, the smell of meadows and hedgerow thick and sweet, the silence of the grass-carpeted countryside broken only by our breathing.

Then he leaned in and kissed me, and my world realigned once more.

———

My first day on the job was as unremarkable as I'd expected it to be. Máire got me there for ten to nine, having spent the entire morning hovering behind me, ready to cajole, to correct, to rush me out the door. My sisters, sleepy, not needed at school until half nine, sat in the back of the car quietly, Lily and Emilia on iPads, Gracie nodding off in her car seat.

—I'll see you here at six. Have a good day. And pull your ponytail out from under your collar for feck's sake.

I did so with an eye-roll that threatened to rupture my optic nerve. Máire handed me my almost-forgotten travel cup full of her fancy coffee – she'd used up two pods of caramel latte just for me – and waved me off into the hardware shop, her palms whiter than her tanned arms, like someone had soaked the skin in half an inch of bleach. I was nervous. I didn't play well with new people, too conscious of saying the wrong thing, of making a social misstep that couldn't be retraced, couldn't be undone. The coffee cup bounced around my tremorous hands, sticky heat sloshing against the lid, leaking from the mouthpiece at the top.

The doors were locked. I could see someone pulling a dolly between the aisles and I knocked on the glass. A tall woman, with jet-black hair and a severe fringe, dropped the dolly handle with a slap and came towards me. She turned the key and let me in.

—New girl.

Nadia's voice, gravelly and shaped by a Baltic tongue, scared me instantly. I followed her like a lost puppy for the rest of the morning as she taught me how to use the till, the card scanner, the ancient-looking clock-in machine in the small staff room that smelled like microwaved vegetable soup and old coffee grounds. She told me to pick my break time every morning and write it in the grid drawn up on a small, dirty whiteboard that hung above the round, laminate breakroom table. Others had already claimed the two slots for 1 p.m., the two slots for 2 p.m. So I jotted *Saoirse* down in the first 3 p.m. slot. Not that it mattered. I wouldn't eat a lunch. I'd drink three coffees and smoke a handful of ciga- rettes and that would keep me conscious until home time. This had always worked in the pub; James would make me a strong cappuccino from the fancy espresso machine and I'd neck it in the fifteen minutes I'd manage to snatch between cleaning piss off bathroom floors, pulling creamy pints of Guinness that made old men's heads wobble with the want, hauling teetering piles of glasses back to the dishwasher, filling lines of shot glasses with vodka and whiskey and tequila and rum, knocking back a shot or two myself. I liked the constant movement. A dead day in the pub was rare but I dreaded them all the same. I missed the pub, I realised, as Nadia set me up restocking boxes of nails in a middle aisle.

—Sort by size. Look, will you? It's written on the bags what the sizes are. 2d go here. 3d go there. 4d after that. That's not enough. Make sure the boxes are full, it's a Monday you know.

I ripped open bag after plastic bag of hard, cold, metal nails, listened to the clink of them hitting off one another as I refilled each box, the glint of the fluorescent lights bouncing off their shiny, unsullied heads, their freshly sharp tips. By eleven I was bored and starving. Lunchtime seemed like it was aeons away. Once the nails were restocked, Nadia pointed me in the direction of the paint aisle. I had to take cans of paint off the dolly one at a time, put a thick strip of parcel tape across the top of every one and then a price tag, before placing it onto the shelf. The price tag gun made me murderous; it gummed and stuck and I kept typing in the wrong price and having to re-tag the paint, and what should have been an hour's job kept me busy and irate for twice that long. After I put the last one on the shelf, a big bucket of landlord's-favourite magnolia, and before Nadia could collar me again, I snuck out the fire exit and lit a big lovely cigarette. I checked my phone. I still had two fucking hours before lunch. There were tears in my eyes. I wanted to run away and never come back. I considered faking a horrible work-related injury; a galvanised shelf falling on me, perhaps, or a nail stuck straight through the palm like the stigmata, or a terrible case of botulism caught from the limescaled coffee machine in the staff room. But I'd never get out of here if I didn't go back in there. I dried my eyes, flicked my butt onto the cracked, broken tarmac and went back to work, but not before sending Charlie a quick text lamenting the state of my affairs. What I got back was a photo of a Honda Civic up on a jack, Charlie's outstretched hand hovering at the side of the photo, covered in grease and dirt and a little blood on the cuticles where the skin was raw and dry from carbolic soap. It kind of annoyed me. Yeah, he *probably* had it worse, but he chose his job. I didn't. Nobody Irish was ever too willing to let me feel sorry for myself. If I broke a toe, somebody else lost a foot in a mowing accident. If my cat went missing, someone else's dog got hit by a car. If I got cancer, somebody's granny was choked with forty tumours and a touch of consumption for good measure. The overarching theme of the Annual Irish Suffering Olympics was *get over yourself, there's worse off than you.*

———

—So what's the plan then?
　—Back to mine? Parents are in Benidorm for the week.
　—Back to Seány's it is.
　—Have we a bag sorted or what?
　—You ring Johnjoe and we'll buy a couple of bottles of wine from the bar. Damo's sound enough, he'll let us have them.

Doireann was clinging to Connor who was giving the orders. She was gazing up at him all doe-eyed and reverential. I thought it was a bit desperate but that might have been the cocaine confidence. I both did and didn't want to clutch onto Charlie the same way. I settled for pulling my jacket a little bit tighter around me as Charlie and Seány took off to get more coke and Doireann and Connor went back into the pub to harangue the barman into selling them six bottles of their cheapest wine. It was 2 a.m. and I'd never felt more awake in my life. All I wanted was more of everything; more drink, more coke, more cigarettes, more people, more dancing, more night. I never wanted the sun to come up again. I did a little spin around with my face up towards the streetlights, and the people around me filing out of the bars gave me looks, but I felt so much more than any of them. I felt more than the entire town with its two dozen pubs and smelly little nightclubs and shops that sold nothing anyone would ever need. I wasn't supposed to be here. That was always the problem.

We walked back to Seány's estate; me, Charlie, Doireann, Seány, Connor, and Doireann's friend Kelsey, who was okay in small doses but really grated on me after a while. She didn't smoke, and when I lit a cigarette she coughed and waved a hand in front of her face, exaggerated and manicured, even though we were outdoors and I wasn't standing next to her. I stuck to the outside of the group and a little ahead of everyone. The town was dead, everyone long gone back to gaffs or bed, taxis piled with people sharing the price of a lift home. Only stragglers remained; a baby-faced couple sucking tongues in the doorway of the travel agents, a very hammered man pissing against the side of McDonald's, girls sitting barefoot on the footpath outside the Italian takeaway eating chips with drunken aplomb. Before I left for London, the streets would be black with drinkers until after the witching hour, screaming, embracing, laughing, fighting. The last good thing about this place was the nightlife and even that was dying. We'd once had three nightclubs; a level of opulence not usually found in towns with a population of only twenty thousand. The best of the three had closed while I was away. The landlord converted it into tiny, expensive apartments that were now filled with *young professionals*; boring people who commuted to Dublin for work every day. Now the other two clubs had to compete over the remaining townies. It was a choice between overpriced drinks and a nice dancefloor, or cheaper drinks and old carpet that smelled like feet. We mostly opted for the overpriced drinks because I always had a naggin in my handbag to top everyone up. No flies on this girl. The further up the town we walked, the more it depressed me. For every two shopfronts in business, a third was shut down, the windows dusty or washed with white emulsion, the innards stripped, a pile of unopened junk mail under the door jambs. I didn't even recognise most of the shops. Boutiques selling cheap clothing at a ridiculous mark-up, chintzy record shops and saccharine boba tea establishments came and went, open for maybe a year before they realised none of us had any interest in being sold utter shite. Nobody had the money for shite. This wasn't a metropolis. The most enduring thing about this town was its proximity to Dublin. I stopped on the bridge and threw a fifty cent coin over my shoulder, making a wish as it landed in the Royal Canal. It was more childish than anything. Someone would just fish it out and spend it eventually. Doireann and Kelsey laughed at the sight of my eyes squeezed shut and my left hand arcing, the coin hitting the still, murky water with a plop.

When we got back to Seány's, his younger brother and some of his friends were already there with music on, the smell of weed seeping out through the cracks of the front door. They looked nearly too young and I felt awkward being such a mess in front of them, the sound of my bank card against the dinner plate almost lurid in their presence. Kelsey looked uncomfortable and left early, her nose in the air. She hugged Charlie goodbye an iota too long and I thought about ripping her arms off and beating her with them. I was getting out of my box a little too enthusiastically. I couldn't keep my eyes still. Doireann dragged me into the kitchen, a hideous late-2000s-burnt-sienna nightmare. She poured me a massive glass of wine and *cheers*ed me so hard the glass shattered and wine went all over the ugly, grainy orange tiling. All we could do was laugh as Charlie picked big lumps of glass out of a pool of chardonnay and Seány frowned, a wad of kitchen roll in one hand to dry it up.

—I'll have to replace that glass before Mammy and Daddy get home.

—Mammy and Daddy? Christ, what are you, six?

Doireann was laughing so hard her knees were knocking together, no breath left in her lungs. Seány shot Charlie a look and all of a sudden his glass-collecting was abandoned and I was being led back to the living room and handed some water. Doireann got away with it. Seány liked her better anyway. Everyone did. She had this flawless way of making her laugh the only sound in the room. She was all straight teeth and shiny legs. She was funny and she could get along with boys just as well as girls. If I liked girls I probably would have been utterly obsessed with her. I could hear her making Seány forget he was ever annoyed with her from my solitary confinement in the living room. Charlie had dropped me into an armchair and gone to do more lines. A joint made its way round to me and he side-eyed me but said nothing. Out of thickness I took five or six hefty pulls and blew them in his direction. I regretted it not long after. But then I had another line and I was okay again, having a grand time, dancing with Doireann and playing stupid drinking games and listening to conversations that jumped from pregnant school friends to Palestinian genocide to the merits of taking mushrooms in a forest. Never mind the nausea, the sweating, the shaky hands and knees. Never mind the bees behind my eyes. Never mind the heart rate going slow then fast then slow again. Never mind the growing urge to jump out the window or talk at a thousand miles an hour about something terrible and awful and traumatic that no one really wanted to hear. Charlie was deliberately ignoring me. I would reach out to touch him, to put a hand on his arm, and he wouldn't move, wouldn't react, only addressing me when I outright said his name. He spoke evenly, but there was a sliver of something hot and shameful in the way he looked at me. The ashtray became a funeral pyre, stacked high with cigarette butts and matches, and dawn broke too soon. By the time the birds began to sing I felt desperate. I had so much anxiety built up inside of me that I thought my veins might burst open and coat the room. Doireann and Connor got a taxi back to his. Charlie and I didn't have the price of a taxi so we slept on the settee, opposite ends, my feet curled up almost into my abdomen, his face turned in towards the couch cushions. We had to suffer through some young fella warbling 'The Green Fields of France' before he succumbed to the daylight. Charlie gave up asking him to shut the fuck up about halfway through the second chorus. I was too wired to sleep still but Charlie eventually began to snore. The last time I looked at the clock, it was a quarter past eight in the morning.

I don't remember falling asleep. The rank heat of Seány's living room made me wake up damp and disoriented. June sunlight burst through the curtains and stung my eyes, but when I turned my face from the window I was met with the dead smell of the night. It was too much. I had to sit up. I sat up and immediately wanted to puke. I needed to lie back down. I couldn't lie back down. I pulled myself across Charlie's now-outstretched legs like a spider, arms reaching to find the floor, to crawl over empty cans and ashtrays and shoes. My legs were bare and dirty-looking; I could feel the debauchery stuck to my skin like gauze, my sweat drying cold and making me shivery. I pulled a random coat over me and searched the pockets for a cigarette. I found a box of Marlboro and a lighter and stood on the back step of the house, hands trembling, a weird lightness in my head. I checked the time. It was only midday. Hadn't slept too long. I needed to go home. The birds in the yard took no heed of me; they were picking through the neat lawn. I wished I was a bird. No bird ever drank the place dry or took a load of drugs and regretted it. They just flew about and occasionally got eaten by bigger animals or milled by cars. That was a trade-off I could accept. I couldn't finish the cigarette. I doused it and brought it inside to the bin. On the counter next to the bin was a half-empty bottle of chardonnay. Before I knew it, the lukewarm wine was halfway down my oesophagus. *Why am I doing this?* The impulse was bizarre, even for me. I was a strict non-believer in imbibing the hair of the dog that bit me. Still, I drained the bottle. Then I panicked and rinsed my mouth with tap water. Then I was drunk again. All within fifteen minutes of waking up. I sat at the cheap pine kitchen table and closed my eyes to the bottles, the cans, the farmhouse kitsch, fingertips on my temples, the room spinning. Naturally, eventually, I was sick in the kitchen sink. Drunk and hungover at the same time. *Can I put that under Achievements on my CV?* I hadn't eaten in over twenty-four hours so I just ran the tap and rinsed away the evidence, the yellow-brown bile tinged with blood from my throat, raw and torn from coke-drip and smoke.

By the time Charlie woke up, I'd assumed the foetal position in an armchair, knees pulled up to my chin, exhausted and beyond ready to leave. I didn't necessarily want to go back to my mother's house, but at least it didn't smell like a dirty ashtray. I wanted Charlie to take me home with him. I wanted him to stroke my hair and let me snake an arm across his chest. I wanted to nap together for hours in a bed that smelled of him. I did not want to ask for any of this, so he dropped me off at Máire's house and then I was sulky as well as hungover. We didn't speak the entire drive. I got out, and before I shut the door, I asked:

—Are you mad at me?

—No, sure why would I be?

—I dunno. I embarrassed you. I'm sorry.

—You didn't embarrass me, it's fine. I'll give you a text later.

His tone was cool and he didn't really look at me. Then he left. I came in to my mother's house quietly, to avoid speaking to anyone. I had a little cry in the shower then, blowing blood and debris out of my nose before drying off, rubbing a palmful of Máire's expensive body butter into my skin and lying on the bed in my towel, contemplating my shit life. I waited until I heard the click of car doors and the rev of an engine on its way out the driveway before venturing downstairs for sustenance. The tell-tale scrunch of my uterus meant my period was arriving imminently; I had limited time to gather supplies and retreat. I filled a hot-water bottle, ignoring the violent tremor in my hands. I made four slices of toast slathered in Nutella and a Thermos full of tea to avoid a second trip to the kitchen. I scrounged two Solpadeine and filled my dad's Harp pint glass full with water. I stopped briefly to pet Max, whose hulking, matted frame shook as he beat his tail off my bare legs. Then I stowed myself away in a cave of blankets, put on ages-old episodes of *Teen Mom*, and tried not to think about killing myself. *Teen Mom* was one of those shows that you'd never admit to another person that you watched, yet it endlessly fascinated me. I could pretend that I cared about its safe sex message, or that I found the statistics behind the rate of teen pregnancy in America unbelievably interesting, but it wasn't really true. I just loved to observe other people's mess. *Teen Mom, Hoarders, Judge Judy*, and other trash TV staples all piqued my interest purely for the nosiness of it. I wanted to see people at their worst. I supposed it made me feel better about myself.

All evening, I telepathically willed my phone to ding. *Just one message. Just one little hi or hey. Anything. Just let me know you're thinking about me too.* It only went off once, a notification for a new Instagram post by Doireann who was out with her old school friends and hadn't invited me, and it annoyed me so much I fucked the phone onto the floor and rolled over, knocking my cold toast crusts all over the bed and the laptop. Charlie was probably out again and hadn't invited me either. Everyone was having a grand old time and I was there rotting and alone because I'd annoyed everyone when I was off it the night before and now nobody would ever want to hang about with me ever again. At least, that was the overarching theme of my internal monologue. My head hurt and my chest hurt and my womb hurt and I was having a terrible time of it altogether. I considered a glass of Máire's good red wine and then remembered my weird chugging incident that morning and decided against it, a flash of panic tickling the back of my neck at the memory. I settled for digging my nails into my arms over and over, crescents of aching red flesh dug into my wrists, my forearms, my elbows. Eventually I fell asleep, and didn't wake again until the next morning.

It was nearly a week before I heard from Charlie again. One line of a message on Saturday afternoon – *wanna come driving tonight??* – and my heart was bursting out of my chest all over again. I'd been in agony, wanting so badly to message him first but petrified he wouldn't respond. Then I'd look needy. I tried not to think about the last time we'd seen each other. Shame swept the feet out from under me when I remembered it. At work, I struggled to focus, the whole thing a perpetual slog, ringing up items and making small talk and brushing floors while trying not to spontaneously combust at the thought of seeing Charlie's remarkable face as he moved it closer to mine. They'd pick me up from Máire's last, everyone else already in the car, smoking and laughing and listening to tunes, usually nineties rap, which we all enjoyed mostly for the phoney feeling of nostalgia for a decade we didn't even really remember. With these little jaunts, we were edging ever closer to date territory. Who knew the back seat of a car could actually be romantic? Connor stuck to the back lanes; it was a bank holiday, and the Gardaí would be out in bigger numbers to catch speeders and drunks and junkies sloppily piloting metal death traps on all the major roads. I watched the countryside slip by out the window, falling asleep under a blanket of lavender, cows lying down in fields and the occasional street lamp flickering the colour of orange peel. Then the ditches bent familiarly, and I realised we were driving out towards my Granny Maher's house. As its mossy roof and squat, popcorned walls appeared above the hedgerow, something like instinct made me say *pull in for a minute.*

The house was, for all intents and purposes, abandoned. My father's crusty little sister Joan had inherited it and had no use for it but was too sentimental to sell it on. She lived permanently in Australia with her daddy-rich, equally crusty husband and their six kids named things like River and Meadow and Sage, all of them with varying degrees of fucked-up teeth and a mother who didn't believe in vaccines. I'd come to the conclusion that she must have taught them to brush with the branches of trees. They only visited once as a family, when I was about seven and there were only three children, and I hated every second of it. I spent the days of my summer break in my grandmother's house; my mother worked and my father worked and nobody else had time for me. Joan and her smelly husband Kit and her grubby kids stayed for three weeks, spreading across my granny's house with their TV accents and unpainted wooden toys and reusable cloth nappies that had to be boiled in a big stew pot on the range so that the whole kitchen developed a light tang of urea. The children weren't allowed to watch cartoons, weren't allowed to eat jelly and ice cream or play the PlayStation or even use my scented markers to colour with. All we could really do was play in the yard, and I quickly grew tired of hearing about how the weather and the trees and the birds and the dirt were different at *their* house. They told me over and over that my name wasn't a real name and that my real name was Sarah. They insisted; *seer-sha* wasn't a name in Australia so obviously I'd misheard my own name and started pronouncing it wrong. It also vexed me, even then, that they had money, like *money*-money, and still they chose to walk and talk and dress and stink like forest people.

When Joan's back was turned, Máire would check the labels on things like her coat or her baby bag or her dusty boots and raise an eyebrow and say things like *unbelievable* and *Kate Spade, seriously* under her breath. Joan put a lot of money into looking like a commune leader. My mother had always been a woman with champagne taste, even when she was on a Dutch Gold budget. At the time we had next to nothing, but still, when in company, I was scrubbed clean and kept neat, no holes in my tights or scuffs on my shoes or lopsided pigtails. I might have looked different at the end of the day but my mother would rather have laid down in the middle of the road and died than send me to anyone's house with unwashed hair and dirty ears. Joan did not feel the same. Granny Maher, whose attention was always devoted to me as I was the only grandchild within a ten-thousand-mile radius, suddenly had four times the grandchildren to dote on, but I wasn't willing to share her. She was the one stable adult in my life. Back in the good old days, when my parents went on benders together instead of separately, they'd leave me at her house, sometimes for three or four days at a time, mobile phones turned off, God knows where. But I didn't care, because Granny loved me. She loved me fiercely and with her whole heart. She kept me fed and warm and never resented me for it. My mother's side of the family didn't really bother with me, didn't know me. Maybe they loved me, but it was out of obligation rather than anything else. Until she died, Granny Maher was the one I ran to when things went wrong.

The only time she raised her voice to me in my whole life was during Joan's visit. My last straw was the biscuit tin. Every afternoon, Granny would produce this big, red tin with a Scottish terrier painted on the front on a background of tartan, and I'd be allowed to pick out two biscuits from the confines. Custard creams, Jammie Dodgers, pink wafers, bourbons, and even the occasional shiny, foil-wrapped Tea

Cake would lie inside, waiting for my small, skinny little fingers to pluck out and devour. But because the other children couldn't have processed sugar, I couldn't have a biscuit. It wasn't fair, Joan said, for her kids to watch me tuck into things they weren't allowed to eat. Then I saw her pull a lemon puff out of her sleeve and shove it straight into her mouth when she had her face turned in towards the refrigerator. That was it. Enraged over the biscuits, and still seething over Granny's less-than-singular attentions, I pinched one of the younger ones – it might have been Meadow, I had a couple of years on her – on the arm, hard, when I thought nobody was looking. I still remember the satisfaction I got from feeling my nails dig into the baby-soft flesh of her dirty, tanned bicep, how the skin turned white, then pink, then red and purple. We bruised just the same. I wanted to do it again, and again and again, until my nails were peeling off my fingers. She squealed like a stuck pig and ran to her mother while I ran to hide under the legs of the dining table. Joan pulled off her shawl, scooped Meadow up and pressed her to the exposed skin of her chest, making clucking sounds and cradling her like a baby, which she most certainly was not. My own mother had stopped picking me up once I started school because I wasn't a baby anymore, and that's the way it was supposed to be. So I hid and Joan cradled and Meadow cried and when Granny emerged from the kitchen at all the fuss, Meadow told Joan and Joan told Granny and Granny grabbed me by the arm of the jumper and dragged me out from under the table.

　　—Don't you ever carry on like that again in my house. Do you hear me?

I did hear her; I couldn't hear anything else. Her voice was loud and shrill, and I instantly felt my cheeks flush and a rush of saltwater in my eyes. I was staring at the floor and she grabbed my chin and tilted it up so our eyes were level.

—Only spoiled brats hurt others for attention. Are you a spoiled brat?

I shook my watery head.

—Get out of my sight.

And then softer:

—Go. Outside. Go on.

As I moped under the open kitchen window I heard them discussing me; *vicious*, Joan said. *Too clever for her own good, always contradicting, always picking at my kids like they're nothing to her, like they're stupid.* Granny said *she's only a child, Joanie, leave her be; you've met her mother.* And then she snapped the window shut and I drifted out of the yard, across the fence and down towards the grove of crooked apple trees to think for the first time about a world without me in it, and what that would look like for everyone I knew.

The answer was always *better.*

The wheels of the car crackled over the gravel as Connor turned them inwards to stop on the soft verge of the ditch.

—This was my granny's house.

—Oh right. That's… nice. Can we pull off again, babes?

—No, hang on, I need to rock a piss anyway.

—Sure fuck it, we'll all have a piss. We deserve it.

We all climbed out a car door each, slapping them shut almost in unison so that the sound was magnified in the quiet country air. I slipped around the back of the house while everyone else found a bush to fertilise. My breath caught in my throat at the sight of the little Virgin Mary statue on the sheltered back step. I lifted her and sure enough the spare key was still there. When I picked it up it left behind a little rust outline on the concrete. Half-expecting the locks to be changed, I didn't really believe it when the latch clicked at the turn of the key. Opening the door, I stepped into the wasteland of a recurring nightmare.

The house, empty now for years, stank of damp and decay. The last time I was here was the day of her funeral. I sat next to my father, whose appearances over those last six weeks had been spotty at best, and drank tea laced with Jameson and shook hands and hid in the bathroom when I had to cry because a Maher didn't cry in front of people, not even the crustiest of us. Joan and her army of children showed up once again at the very end of Granny's life, after she'd lost the ability to speak full sentences or even keep her eyes open for longer than five minutes at a time. We gathered in the Cluain Lir suite of the hospital where they shunt the elderly off to die in peace. They don't even bother with life support; just oral morphine, nasal oxygen, and maybe a bag of saline, if the patient's veins can support the constant freezing push of liquid. Joan put me out of the high-backed chair next to Granny's bedside so that she could lean over her and play the distraught daughter, hawing into her sleeping, pained face with her disgusting herbal breath. If she gave that much of a shit then why was it me that had been sitting in that chair, alone, every day for a fortnight? Her children, ranging from sixteen to six at that stage, were sleepy, jet-lagged, and bored. I couldn't believe she'd trooped them all into the hospital at once. I slipped a

Silk Cut Blue out of Granny's coat pocket, along with her lighter, and excused myself.

She'd been alone in her house on a Friday night when the tumours finally made themselves known, sitting in her armchair, ashtray and matches and Silk Cut resting on the floral arm, her crochet needles in her lap, the telly turned to RTÉ 1 for *The Late Late Show*. Dad didn't find her until it was really too late for them to fix anything at all. When he came into the house the next morning, she was still in the armchair, black blood spattered and coughed up all over her jumper, unable to catch a breath, unable to even reach the phone to call someone. The hospital did the scans, considered surgery, offered chemo, but to no avail. Granny said *no thanks, I've been alive long enough*. And that was that. They sent her home but she'd had to be admitted again three weeks later, and this time we knew there'd be no going home again. I'd been skipping school to sit with her in the hospital, only going home when Dad finished work in the evenings and came in to take over. Eventually the nurses started doing things like making me tea and toast or getting me a Dairy Milk from the vending machine; the nicer they became, the closer to the end I knew we were. I couldn't bear to leave my grandmother there like that alone, to step out of the hospital and into my school uniform and pretend everything was okay and nobody was dying. Instead, I sat and listened to the degradation of her speech centres, watched her first become unable to walk, then stand, then sit up unaided. I held her hand tightly to stop her from flailing her purple-black arms as she moaned in pain, ghosts appearing at her bedside. Occasionally her eyes would spring open and she would eke out a name, Molly or Hildie or Johnny (my grandfather, who died about three months before I was born), mostly Jesus Christ, *please Jesus forgive me my sins* over and over and over until it started to become more of a moan than an incantation. I read her Wordsworth from her own childhood copy of his poetry, examined with reverence the tiny notes written in the margins when she fell asleep. A day or two before the end, she sat up, looked at me, and said clear as a bell, *please, I just want to be happy.* Then she went back to sleep. That was the last thing she ever said to me. Might have been the last thing she ever said.

Those words rang in my head every single day of my life after. I thought about them first thing in the morning, last thing at night, mid-daydream, mid-nightmare. They were my poltergeist, rearranging the furniture inside of my body, knocking things over, shattering them. They hung between my ears as big and bright as a blood moon as I moved around her kitchen now; all the cupboards were bare of anything worth something. Only mismatched mugs and plastic cutlery sat around, dusty and unwanted. Her big cabinet, once full of her wedding gifts, porcelain plates and crystal flutes and gold-rimmed cups, sat empty, rotting and mouldy, one of the panes of glass shattered all along the brown tile floor. I could hear mice in the walls, smell their musk laden into the foundations of the house. Joan had inherited everything, stripped it for parts, and left it to rot.

My father, like me, clearly hadn't been here since the funeral either. I closed my eyes and could still smell the hidden whiskey breath, see the tilt of his body as we shook hands with strangers over and over and over, his posture becoming more and more hunched with every mouthful of spiked tea, my own mouth numb and rubbery from the Jameson. My mother had dropped me off at the funeral home that morning and driven away, no interest in mourning a woman who wouldn't have mourned her. My cousins had avoided me, or maybe I had grown a thicket of brambles around myself and fixed them into a cage so that everyone stayed away from me. I felt it creep across me again like the shadow of a bare tree as I moved deeper and deeper into the house, through the hallway with the now-dirty, moth-chewed carpet, into the living room where the neighbours had circled her open casket like a museum attraction, staring down at her waxen face, the eyelids and the lips glued shut by the funeral home, garish makeup smeared on her cold skin. She'd never worn so much as a layer of Chapstick and they'd done her up like a streetwalker. Before they loaded her into the hearse to drive her home, I burst into tears and demanded they clean it off her. My father shushed me as Joan cut me in two with a look. Then he bundled me into the passenger seat of his Transit van where he gave me a fag and had me pick out horses in the newspaper. It worked, oddly enough. I'd stopped crying by the time we pulled in ahead of the hearse at Granny's house, and I didn't cry about her again until I was on the plane to England.

From the kitchen, I heard the creak of the back door, followed by a skid and the bang of shinbone on wood.

—Shit.

Charlie. I wanted to speak out, so he'd know where to go, but my voice box was crystallised. He found me anyway, in the dark, in the dust and the cobwebs and the death and the decay, and took a second to look at me strangely before saying:

—You alright?

I thought of all the things I wanted to say; all the hurt inside of me that stayed perpetually hidden in the shallows like basking sharks, thought of how his face would change as the words formed in the air between us, first into a slight gape of shock, and then into a withered mask of pity and maybe even disgust at how pathetic I was, really, behind it all. So instead I said *yeah, grand* and let him take my hand.

I put the key under Mary and got back into the car and drank another three bottles of cider, and by the time we got to Connor's house later that night, I had a good buzz on. Thoughts of my grandmother and hospitals and families and death had been placed on mute, suspended in a sheen of fermented apple. Connor's parents had a large galvanised shed at the back of the garden, half of which they'd let him turn into a sort of clubhouse. One half stored tools, bikes, a wall of dried turf, and a ride-on John Deere lawn mower covered in a big green tarp. Connor's side had a pool table, the green felt pooling and ripped in spots, an old TV with a smattering of dead pixels in the top left corner, and two battered sofas. They turned out to be deceptively comfortable. Eventually, after much graceless fondling and innuendo between them, Connor and Doireann disappeared into the main house, giggling as they tiptoed into the dark. Charlie and I never spoke about the weekend before, and eventually all thought of it was gone from me. I'd miraculously managed to fix it by pretending it never happened. Charlie kissed me, properly and with no restraint; no hiding in the back of the car or stealing a minute in the hallway of the nightclub or all the other increasingly horny and frustrating ways in which we had been touching one another since we'd met. If either of us had lived alone then we would have had sex by now, absolutely no question there. But we both had younger siblings that we shared bedroom walls with, and neither of us was comfortable with potentially traumatising anyone.

Within moments I was in his lap, and not long after that, we lay back on the couch, glossy and breathless. He'd slid a hand between my legs while inside of me and drawn runes with the tips of his fingers, my voice an incantation, spellcasting. When the haze began to lift from me, when my skin started to turn cold and seed gooseflesh, I pulled my dress back down and my knickers back up and lit a cigarette, passed it to him when he was finished redoing his jeans.

—Well that was quick.

—Who's got forty minutes for an orgasm these days?

—Touché. Enjoy yourself, jelly legs?

I looked down; my legs were, indeed, shaking slightly, although I suspect that had more to do with the cold of the shed than the orgasm, whose rosy aura was leaving me at lightning speed. I didn't place much personal value on sex. It was, usually, something done *to* me as opposed to something I did. Although he did just become the first man to make me cum unaided, which was another fat green checkmark in the Charlie ledger.

—Eugh, what'll I do with the johnny?

—I dunno. Here, I've a tissue.

He wrapped the used condom up in the crumpled Kleenex dug out of the bottom of my handbag and handed it back to me like it was covered in killer bees.

—Men are so strange. It came out of you, it's not poison.

—Exactly. I got it out of me, now I don't want it anywhere near me.

—But you'd expect me to swallow it no problem, wouldn't ya?

—Well it'd be nice, but I'm all for a woman making her own choices.

—Maybe I'll *choose* to leave this johnny in your shoe when you're not looking.

—Don't even mess.

I held up the tissue, wrapped around latex, inside of which sat one perfect half of the beginning of all humanity, and started approaching him with it until he was pressed against the back of the sofa and I was cackling like a witch on bath salts.

—Funny, aren't ya?

—I'm Carol fuckin' Burnett, babe.

—Well you laugh like Jimmy Carr.

—Fuck off.

He laughed then, and kissed me, and kissed me again, and again, and we spent the rest of the night knotted together like a scribble of ink, jackets thrown over us against the cold of the shed, smoking joints and casting YouTube videos onto the battered TV. He played me songs and told me why he loved them; this one for his mother, that one for a summer spent in Greece, a third one for the time he tried to kill himself with an overdose and woke up two days later – teenage angst, he was quick to assure me, after a girlfriend dumped him. It embarrassed him to speak about it, I could see the blush creep across him, but he told me anyway, and I appreciated it. In turn, I spoke of my grandmother; how she had died, and what that had done to me, but I told it in more of a based-on-real-events, straight-to-TV movie sort of way rather than a horribly depressing sort of way; I was still scared he'd pity me instead of fancy me. Nevertheless, we started to understand one another. Tendrils of him took root inside my chest like wallflowers in the crevices of brick, filling up old cracks and missing mortar. I would water him, sun him, tear myself down to make sure he grew. This I already knew even before I loved him.

It was just my way.

———

July arrived, loud and shining. I woke up on my Saturday off to a room washed in gorgeous yellow light and a text from Doireann. *Lake later bbz? Desperate for a tan that didn't come out of a bottle.* I sent back a thumbs up. It was nice to start the day with a plan. I didn't like spending my days off in Máire's house. She was sure to rope me into something I didn't want to do. As I ate my breakfast, a bowl of soggy, sugar-glazed cornflakes and a strong cup of tea, my mother sat across from me and picked at some loose skin on her bottom lip. She held all her stress in her shoulders, scrolling on her phone compulsively. She was irritating me.

—Everything okay?

—Yeah. No. I don't know. Have you plans today?

I paused, mouth full of cereal. There was a vulnerability to her question. I swallowed hard and the mushy cornflakes slid down my throat in a big lump.

—Do you need me for something?

—I have to go and visit Mammy. It's my turn.

Granny Lynch was formidable; not at all like my Granny Maher. Granny Lynch had clear favourites among her children and grandchildren, and both my mother and I were nowhere near the top of either list. My mother was certainly her least favourite daughter, and I sat somewhere in the second half – depending on the day. I suspected if I'd been born a boy I might have worked my way up the ranks to golden grandchild, might have been slipped ten-euro notes on my way out of her house, might have been given the bigger slice of Viennetta after dinner, but as it stood, I was a girl, and I looked too much like my father.

—I'll come. What time?

The halls of the nursing home were cool, mirage-like; getting out of Máire's car, I'd had to unstick myself from the seat, but once indoors, gooseflesh cropped up on the outsides of my arms. Granny Lynch was sitting upright in a pink plasticky leather chair, her hands folded in her lap like withered lily blossoms, staring out the window of her room and into the car park. The windows had no handles. I could feel my mother's tension, the space between us taut, strained with it. For my own part, I felt removed. The carer, a small, plump woman named Martina who'd met us past the keypad-locked door in reception, announced our arrival.

—Concepta, you've visitors! I'll go and fetch a pot of tea. She's in good form today; she's a flower, grows best in the sunshine. Isn't that right, Concepta?

My grandmother looked like she might spit at her. Martina left the room and my mother and I stood there like discarded traffic cones; I flinched first, moving to sit on the hospital bed pushed against the wall, the metal frame squeaking under my weight. It had my grandmother's own comforter on it, crocheted painstakingly in oranges and browns and ochres. My mother took the chair opposite Granny, first kissing her on the forehead and squeezing her shoulders awkwardly with one arm.

—Is that you, Imelda?

—No, Mammy, it's me. Máire.

—I know that.

Granny had started rocking almost imperceptibly and my mother was mimicking her body language, hands in her lap, slight hunch.

—Which one is this? My eyesight is gone very bad. They won't let me see a doctor.

—You know who that is, Mammy. That's Saoirse, my eldest.

—The lesbian?

I bit my tongue to keep from laughing.

—How are you, Granny?

—I might as well be dead as in here.

Martina came back with a pot of tea, steaming, and three little cups with saucers and spoons. She put the tray on the table with the teapot next to my mother, as far away from Granny as she could get it.

—When is Assumpta coming?

Assumpta was Granny's sister. She'd been dead for six years.

—Mammy, we've been over this. Assumpta passed away, remember?

—I knew that.

My mother looked pained. It fell awkwardly silent. We drank the tea and Martina turned on *Home and Away* on the television mounted to the wall. I submerged myself in ambient noise; the hum of the air conditioning, the low rumble of Australian accents, the beeping of machinery somewhere down the hall, the sterile shuffling of rubber-soled shoes on linoleum, and other families convening in the common area, laughing quietly, enjoying each other's company. Then, my grandmother's voice like a knitting needle through an eyeball.

—You are the greatest shame of my life.

She was looking directly at my mother, no longer so frail, sitting taller, staring at her, unblinking, even in the harsh chink of sunlight falling into her face, giving her thin, white hair a shock of yellow. Her eyes were screaming blue, pupils like pin pricks, watering in the corners. My mother sat, stunned for a moment, and I thought she might actually cry. Instead, she calmly, calmly, gathered up her handbag and excused herself for a breath of air. I didn't move to follow her; I knew she wouldn't appreciate it. Instead, I took her seat, and by that point Granny had looked away again, back out the window.

—When is Assumpta coming?

—She's away today, Granny, she has an appointment.

—Oh, that's a shame. What do you do again?

—I'm just home from England.

—You're very like my Máire when she was small. Very like her.

No one ever really said that to me, least of all Concepta.

—Do you think so?

—Yeah, yeah, very like her, in the eyes and the chin. She broke my heart, that one. Went off and got herself pregnant, hardly out of her school uniform so she was. Broke her mother's heart.

—Ah, we all make mistakes.

—She did it to hurt me. Then she put me in here. The doctor won't even see me.

—Do you want another cup of tea?

—You'll take me home. You were always a good girl. You pull the car around and I'll grab my bag.

She made no move to get up and neither did I; I just tipped the last of the teapot into our mugs, and she kept looking out into the car park where my mother was now sitting, legs swung out of the driver's seat of her car, sunglasses on, hand at her mouth.

—Where are we, exactly?

—What do you mean?

—I mean I know where we are… but where do you think we are?

My impulse was to tell her the truth, but she was suffering enough.

—We're at a B&B, so you can get some rest, remember?

—Oh yeah. It's nice, is it?

—Lovely. Sure can't you see the flowerbeds there?

—Oh yeah.

She kept her eyes out the window and it was only then that I got a lump in my throat. I drained my mug and got up to say goodbye, hugged her the way my mother did, felt her bird-like bones rub together under the breadth of my palm.

On the drive home, Máire was silent again, kept her sunglasses on. Her bottom lip was split and weeping blood, which she periodically ran her tongue over. I reached across the centre console and put my hand on her hand as it braced the steering wheel. It felt foreign, like the first time you say hello in a new language.

—She's gone horrid bad, isn't she? Breaks my heart.

—Oh, she has her moments, I bet.

—She thinks it was me that put her in there. I had nothing to do with it, it was all Philomena. But she was always the favourite so of course I'm getting the blame instead. As usual. Light two smokes there.

I did as I was bid, handed her one, rolled down my window further. She picked up speed on the dual carriageway and the wind dried the sweat to my skin.

—And what can I even do about it? It's not like I can tell her to fuck off. Half the time I wonder if she's putting it all on so she doesn't have to pretend to like me. That's terrible, isn't it? That's a terrible thing to think.

—I think you're entitled to feel your feelings.

The wind continued to billow in the windows, and I relaxed back onto the seat, cool now from the breeze, watching Lough Owel stretch out to the left, only partly wishing I'd just gone to the lake instead.

When I left the house that evening, it was getting late; the amber haze of sunset was permeating the kitchen, setting all my mother's marble countertops ablaze. She was buried on her end of the sofa, glass of pinot noir in one hand, remote control in the other, all the curtains pulled and *EastEnders* on the television. Phil Mitchell's fat, puce head loomed from the darkness, cockney accent breaking the silence she'd drawn. The girls were with JJ, visiting his mother. My sisters would come home later with sticky faces and pockets holding crumpled-up five-euro notes, sleepy from a day of being loved. I wouldn't be there. I said goodbye to Máire and she didn't respond. Already the wine glass was tilting dangerously to the left, threatening to bleed onto crushed grey velvet. I shut the door quietly on the way out and checked for the spare key under the potted aloe before I left. Charlie picked me up, as usual, at the end of the road. He grabbed my hand and kissed the back of it.

—How was your day?

—Grand. My family were as doting as ever.

—I've a bottle of wine for ya in the cooler. The one with the kangaroo on it.

—You know me too well.

The shore of the lake was littered with towels and outstretched bodies, limbs tanned and glowing in the dying light, splashes and shrieks of elation splitting the hazy air as people jumped from the rickety diving board. We perched next to Charlie's friends; I drank my wine straight from the bottle, and after a while Doireann showed up and we ventured into the shallows together. The surface of the lake fluttered like dyed silk, and as I walked deeper the sharp pebbles turned to dark silt under my bare feet. Charlie watched me from the shore, gazing at my milk-bottle skin, smoke tumbling from his lips like water; when I turned to face the horizon I could feel his eyes on me. But the sunset was calling me deeper still, and I paddled out until my toes hung above the void, wine-drunk and buoyant.

—Saoirse, come back in a bit.

Doireann, still standing waist-deep, sounded annoyed with me. I kept myself afloat, algae brushing against my leg, the sun's last light sinking ahead. Soon, Charlie's voice joined Doireann's, alarm growing between the syllables of my repeated name.

With a last deep breath, I ducked under.

———

The last week of July I had the house to myself; Máire and JJ were taking the girls on a sun holiday. Not to any of the usual destinations; Turkey or the Algarve or somewhere bound to be awash with Irish bars and British tourists. No, no; my mother had chosen a villa in the South of France. Who would've thought a quarry foreman made enough for French villas and business-class plane tickets? Their financial situation confused me and Máire kept the numbers close to her chest, if she even knew them at all. I'd seen her pull out the MasterCard from the back of her purse more than once already; she'd bought two Bruce Springsteen Gold Circle concert tickets the morning they went on sale and left the card sitting on the kitchen counter. It was in JJ's name. I thought she was pathetic and a hypocrite for that.

She had a job, why did she need him to pay for everything? Growing up, she'd drilled it into me that I was never to rely on a man to give me anything except hardship and here she was, hanging off her husband's purse strings.

My mother had been asking me to child-mind on my off-days while she went to work – it was only Tuesday and Thursday mornings before JJ's mother came to pick them up for the afternoon, and it got me in Máire's good books, but it was starting to exhaust my patience. There are only so many episodes of Disney shows one childless adult woman can sit through, and I was rapidly approaching that cut-off point. Weed would've made it more tolerable, as it made most things in my life more tolerable. But I would never get stoned on the mornings I had to babysit, lest something catastrophic happen on my watch. I was afraid I'd take one pull of a joint and *boom*: Lily would fall down the stairs or Gracie would pull a pot of boiling water down on herself or Emilia would escape the house and get a thump of a car, and then I'd be pulled aside in the hospital and they'd smell the grass off me and my mother's kids would be taken by Social Services and I'd be the worst cunt that ever walked the streets of Ireland.

On the weekend they were due to leave, I could hardly contain my excitement. Work was a breeze; I smiled at the elderly and made Nadia coffee, which she sniffed at with her eyes narrowed before drinking. I reorganised all the nail boxes according to size and brand. I dusted the counter before I closed at six and fought the urge to skip out the door. Charlie was waiting for me; I shivered at the stretch of his smile, the auburn stubble spattered on his cheek and, suddenly self-conscious, pulled my hair out of its bun and let it fall across one shoulder. I checked myself in the car mirror, shielding my eyes from the dazzle of the late sun. I was rosé pink. Charlie put the car in gear before laying his hand on my leg, turning the flesh hot.

—How was your day, sweets?

—Good. Grand. Flew by. How was yours?

—Ah, nothing to report.

The girls were getting ready for bed when I got in; their plane to France was at seven in the morning and my mother was determined to have three obedient, well-rested darlings to fly with. In the hallway was a small mountain of luggage, all colour coordinated, all hard plastic shell, all tagged in my mother's neat hand. I dropped my backpack and kicked off my shoes next to the door, the cool hardwood of the floor shocking on my sore and swollen feet. Máire appeared in the kitchen doorway to check I had my shoes off before grunting a hello and disappearing again. She was putting snack packs together for the trip to the airport and the subsequent wait; carrot sticks all cut to exactly equal length, little tubs of creamy hummus, kids' organic yoghurt cups, four squares of high-end milk chocolate, and a small bottle of filtered water from her Brita tap. When her back was turned I snatched a lump of chocolate from the open packet and popped it in my mouth, careful not to chew. It melted quickly, coating my teeth and tongue, staining them cocoa brown.

—Do you need me to go over the house rules again?

I shook my head, mouth still cemented shut.

—And you'll be here when they come to switch the electricity meter?

—Mmhm.

—Between nine and three on Thursday?

—Mmm.

—And you won't light the fire when we're gone?

—Nnng.

—I'm just very precious about that floor in there, you know.

Code: she didn't trust me not to scorch that floor in there. I poured a glass of orange juice and rinsed it around my mouth, the bitter citrus eradicating the cloying taste of the chocolate. I swallowed hard before answering her.

—I won't light the fire. It's roasting anyway.

—Promise me.

—I promise. Jesus.

Twenty-three years of life and she still thought I was incapable of doing the simplest of tasks to meet her ever-fluctuating bar of standards. The only thing worse than following her arbitrary house rules for the week would be to be stuck in a sweltering villa in Nice following her arbitrary house rules for the week. They had invited me – Lily, Emilia, and Gracie specifically, their little hands clapped together in a pleading motion as they regaled me with promises of sandcastles, aquariums, and ice-cream floats – but I politely turned them down. To begin with, I had no holiday money of my own and, despite my mother's blasé frivolity with his wages, I wasn't comfortable with JJ funding me for the week. And then the aforementioned alone time was suddenly dangling in front of me, a juicy carrot to keep me plodding along. I was certain I saw my mother's shoulders relax when I said no, and I knew I was doing the right thing.

When I was a child, we'd never gone on a foreign holiday. My first plane ride was the one I took to London when I emigrated. We never had the money to go further than Salthill in Galway or Bundoran in Donegal, and when we got there my mother watched every euro spent with increasing anxiety. Still, she always did her best with me. She took me to rock pools to pet starfish and gather pretty pearlescent seashells for my bedroom windowsill at home. She brought me to the arcade and, particularly adept at claw games, won me a dozen stuffed animals with a tenner. She'd braid my hair before bed so it would be wavy the next day, perfect for lying in the shallows and pretending I was a mermaid. I'd sing all the songs from *The Little Mermaid*, specifically 'Part of Your World', with my legs pressed together and my feet flat out to the sides like a fishtail, slathered head to toe in a layer of factor-fifty that gathered loose sand like pebbledash on my skin. My mother, browning like a nut in the sun, mostly watched me from her perch on a huge, blue beach towel gifted to her from Hawaii by her jet-setting spinster auntie, her hair blowing into her face from the perma-breeze of an Irish beach, only looking away when she had to tan her front and even then sitting up regularly to check on me. My father was there on and off; mostly in whatever pub was nearest to the hotel or filling a slot machine with the following week's bill money. Once, he'd come to the aquarium with us in Galway. He picked me up so I could pet the rays swimming by. It was one of the best memories I had. It hurt me to think of it; a perfect little round bead of recollection sitting in the middle of my brain like a tumour. I shook my head vigorously, uttered a little *no*, and went to find my sisters.

All three were on the couch in their pyjamas quietly watching the TV, and from the doorway I marvelled at my mother's ability to run a household like the army. I went to my room, found some hair ties and a brush, and came back to the living room. One by one I plaited their hair; two plaits for Lily, two plaits for Emilia, one for Gracie because her hair was shorter, and when I was done I looked up to see Máire standing where I had been moments before.

—Do you want to put them to bed for me? I've a few bits to do still.

—Oh yeah. Sure. After this one?

An ancient episode of *Hannah Montana* was on, one I'd seen before, and it was maybe ten minutes from the ending.

—Yeah. Thanks.

She left us then. When the episode was over I rounded them up, Gracie on my hip, although she was getting a little big for that, and put them to bed, tucking them in at the sides, turning on nightlights, kissing foreheads, closing wardrobe doors. I pulled down the blackout blinds and left the doors open a little crack, on request, and when it was all done, I felt like crying. I didn't know why. I checked my period tracker while I rolled a joint; weeks away from a premenstrual breakdown. Just one of those things. On my way out to smoke, Máire stopped me in the kitchen.

—Thanks for that. I'm the one doing all the last minute holiday bits, as usual. JJ wouldn't even fold a pair of shorts for himself.

—Why don't you just let him face the consequences?

—Ah, he works very hard.

—So do you.

She looked at me. There was a softness, a sadness there. It hurt my chest. I had to look away. In a small voice, she said:

—Do you want to watch a film with me?

We put on one of our old favourites, *What Ever Happened to Baby Jane?* I sat on the floor with my back to her, hugging my knees in the monochrome glow. Before she met JJ, films were always our thing. My mother loved the classics. I'd seen *Gone with the Wind, Casablanca,* and *All About Eve* before I'd seen a Muppets movie. As she sat behind me, she pulled the hair tie out of my hair and began to brush it out. My scalp tingled and pricked, the blood rushing back to the follicles. The tension dissipated from my body, seeped out of my bones.

—Did you know they hated each other?

—Yeah. Makes the movie even better.

Máire split my hair down the centre and began to plait it, one side and then the other, perfect symmetry, one braid a mirror of the other.

—Now all my girls will have mermaid hair tomorrow.

I stayed looking ahead, gaze fixed on Bette Davis, heart twisting and breaking inside of me.

————

I was still awake when they gathered themselves and left for the airport, but I stayed in bed, listening to the sleepy movements of my sisters as they were rounded up for take-off. Gracie was crying at one stage, her weepy little voice trickling through the hallways, and then Máire told her to *stop acting like a baby; babies don't get to go on aeroplanes.* And the house remained voiceless after that. Once the sound of JJ's jeep disappeared from earshot, I got up, had a smoke out the back, left the butt on the step, and brought Max back to bed with me. The smell of his coat was pungent but I just threw my dressing gown over him and rolled onto my side, drifting off to the gentle beat of his tail on the duvet. I dreamt about being lost in the airport, moving through molasses, blind to the exit doors, and woke up with Max across my legs and the bedsheet over my face. *Happy Sunday.* I was working until six; Charlie was going to drop me in and bring me home and that thought alone was what got me out of the bed and into a respectable state. He picked me up at twenty past eight, a takeaway cup sitting in what I had come to know as my cup holder, although I'd never say it out loud. Still, this was very coupley behaviour, and it made me sickeningly giddy. I internalised it, reducing it to jiggling my right leg compulsively until he put his hand on it, making it even worse.

—Any plans for tonight?

—Bubble bath, big smoke, bottle of my mother's expensive pinot. You?

—Gonna head round to Connor's for a game of poker. Even though I'm dogshite at it.

—Really? Show us your poker face then.

He cocked one eyebrow, angled his chin downwards, and gave me a creepy little tight-lipped grin. We both burst into a laugh and, as it died down, I wondered if I should ask him to stay over with me. But the term self-care implied solitude and that's what I needed; space to think my thoughts without interruption, to come up with some sort of a plan to dig my life out of the bog hole before it was sucked in and pickled in peat.

I lasted approximately four hours.

He dropped me home after work and even before I got out of the car I felt anxious; I tried to pinpoint the source, identify the thought that made my stomach lurch in a way that said *that's the one*, but nothing. Just a general and all-encompassing sense of imminent doom. Charlie noticed, asked if I was okay as I grabbed my handbag out of the footwell, and even though I nodded and smiled, I so desperately wanted him to say *I'll cancel poker and stay here with you*. But he didn't, and I wouldn't ask. Every time life gave us a chance to get closer, he seemed to pull away on reflex. Either that or he was entirely oblivious. I thought of his face again that night in Seány's. The look he gave me, like he could just about make out the worst part of me before I managed to shroud it again.

As soon as I shut the door of the house the anxiety escalated to palpitations, and I shook as I poured a glass of Máire's wine. My breath was an irregular flutter in the back of my throat, escaping me. I freed Max from the confines of the utility room and lay on the floor next to him, worrying the hair off his back with my panicky, sweaty-handed petting, and tried to control my breathing. The kitchen tile was cold; I peeled off my jeans and let my sticky legs press against it, which was more helpful than anything else I'd tried so far. I stayed there for fifteen minutes. Max stayed by me, panting, tail wagging gently.

Once I could breathe again, I stood up, let the blood rush back to my feet, grabbed the wine, and plodded up to my room. As I stripped down, rolled a joint, and ran a bath, I drank, and half the bottle was gone by the time I stepped into the hot, bubbly water, the skin of my feet prickling. Smoke mingled with steam and my head swam pleasantly in the lavender haze, the muscles of my neck unclenching. My heart slowed down and I sank into the bath, deeper and deeper until the breath from my nostrils made ripples on the surface. I was safe there, submerged, insulated, in utero. I fell asleep, and when I woke up, the water was stone cold. A voile panel of darkness had fallen outside the window and the hand that held the joint had fallen into the bath. The joint skin disintegrated into the water and chunks of tobacco and weed floated above my fingers. I checked my phone; twenty past ten. I climbed out, limbs heavy and waterlogged, ducked under the heat of the shower briefly to make sure I didn't die of pneumonia, and pulled on my dressing gown before staring at Charlie's name in my phone, chewing my thumb nail, agonising. The house was painfully empty; every noise I made seemed to bounce around the walls before clinging to my back like burdock. I typed messages and then erased them – *hey, how's poker going? you busy later on tonight? wanna come over and make sure I don't kill myself? or maybe watch a movie or ask me to be your girl-friend or profess your love or something idc what we do?* I locked the phone and then unlocked it; I checked his Instagram and found nothing. I went downstairs and got more wine and put a bag of popcorn in the microwave and let the dog out for a piss. I unlocked the phone, again, and opened our message thread, again. As I was about to hit send on a text that said *pls come stay the night with me I'm scared lmao* the phone rang, and I jumped so violently I dropped it on my foot. It was Charlie; I let out a little hiss of pain before

I answered. He was a bit drunk; I could hear it on him, a dreamy, cloudy inflexion to his words that made my pulse quicken.

—All my money is gone.

—But your poker face was so strong. I'm shocked.

—Me too. Care to soothe my stinging ego?

Before he landed at the house, I necked the wine, shaved my legs, and had a talk with myself in the bathroom mirror. *Don't be a clinger. Don't annoy him. Don't dare ask him to stay tomorrow night; if he wants to, he'll bring it up. And for fuck's sake, don't say anything cringy.* Then I gave myself a quick, stingy slap on each cheek for good measure, and for a little natural blush, before I greeted him at the door. He was leaning against the door jamb like the hottie neighbour in a nineties teen sitcom, hair falling in his eyes, a grin on his face, and the gold strobe of the porch light bouncing off him like a halo.

—Well.

—Howaya.

Then we kissed, and we didn't stop kissing the entire way up the stairs to my room, which made the stairs very difficult to navigate but we managed it well enough. He smelled like beer and hotboxing and petrol and his aftershave, and when we had sex I buried my face in his neck, inhaling him, trying to decant the essence of him, to make him a part of me on a molecular level. Afterwards, while he lay in the reddish glow of my lamp, the bedsheet pulled across one hairy leg and the other dangling from the bed, I sat, bottomless, on the windowsill and rolled a joint out of his grinder.

—Whose stuff is this? It smells nice.

—Johnjoe's. It is nice but I fucking hate having to get off him. Have to go into the house and pretend we're mates for an hour until he'll give me the bag.

—Well at least all he wants from you is a bit of chat. I go into a dealer's house alone and I've got my house keys tucked between my knuckles.

—That won't help you. Get yourself one of them spiky keyrings. Jab the cunts right between the ribs. I'll teach you how to throw a punch.

He waved a languid fist in the air. I laughed and then sputtered on a lungful of smoke.

—So this is your room. I have to say, it's not what I expected.

—Well what did you expect?

—I dunno. Purple. Art. Chaos. The lamp is nice though.

—The lamp is the only thing in here that's actually mine.

—Makes sense.

—My mother hates it.

—Well she clearly has terrible taste then.

—You have no idea. The bedsheets were white satin when I got here. Then I got makeup on them and she downgraded me to them grey ones.

—Jesus, don't let her meet me so. I've constantly got dirt somewhere.

—Do you want to meet her?

My question hung there like the joint smoke. He wasn't looking at me.

—Sorry, that was a stupid question.

—I just didn't think we were at that stage. But I'll meet your mam. If you want me to.

—Maybe not. She's kind of mean. She'll definitely be mean to you.

I climbed back in the window and left the moon behind, passing him the joint, running a finger across his forearm where a faded streak of black motor oil ran the length of his ulna. Then I kissed his wrist, felt his blood sing under my lips, followed it up into the crook of his elbow, fought the urge to say something romantic, climbed on top of him and used my hips to spell it out instead.

To my utter joy, although I hid it beneath a coy smile, Charlie offered to stay the next night, and the night after that, and eventually we ended up spending the whole week together in my mother's house, drinking IPAs and cooking pasta and watching movies and walking Max in the evenings, curling up together at night in my bed like cats, heads pressed together, hands interlocked, the whole room smelling of sex and smoke. I was a touch-driven person, it turned out. When he'd circle my waist from behind as I stirred sauce around a pot, or play with my hair as my head lay in his lap, or run a rough finger up my bare spine while we fucked, it satisfied some deep, unseen part of me. He switched my soul on. He was my heaven. We were playing house, I knew that. But I was more than happy to pretend at being a long-term live-in couple with all of the passion and none of the crushing responsibility, no rows over unpaid bills, no compromising food taste for vegan options, no passive-aggressive dish-washing or bed-making. It was wonderful, and nothing at all like living with James, who seemed like more and more of a prick the more distance I got from him. James and I never got that honeymoon phase. We were domesticated before we ever so much as touched off one another. I got bitter when I thought about it too much. I'd unblocked and reblocked James for the last time; the temptation to doom-scroll was strong, but my infatuation with Charlie was stronger.

The day before my family returned I aired out the whole house with a face like a slapped arse. I stripped the bedsheets, vacuumed the floor, bleached the bathroom, soaked the pan we'd burned steak to the night before, erasing all evidence of *us* from every room. We had lit the fire a couple of nights, despite Máire's warning. The cloudless nights brought a chill with them, and the fire added to the romance of it all. I emptied the ashes and hid the bag in the bottom of the wheelie bin. That morning, Charlie, sensing my devastation, gave me his hoodie when he dropped me off at work. It had his smell. I put it on, pulled the collar up around my chin. Once his car had driven away I had to smother a scream with cigarette smoke and peppermint tea, idling outside the doors of the hardware shop, simultaneously hating being outside and dreading going inside.

Money was becoming a real hindrance. Part time in retail didn't stretch incredibly far. We were all planning on going to a local music festival in September and I hadn't even had the lump sum for my ticket; Charlie had bought it for me and I insisted on paying him back. So at the start of August I stopped going out with Doireann on Fridays and picked up extra weekend shifts, partly to dull my fear of missing out, mostly to make sure I could pay Charlie back quickly. I hated owing anything to anyone, especially someone I was close to. It complicated things. It created a power imbalance.

So lucky me got to sweep floors and mix paint for the last handful of sunny weekends of the year, working three sets of Saturdays and Sundays in a row. By the final weekend of the summer, I was richer financially but poorer in the will to live. I hadn't seen Doireann even once in person all August – between her family holiday to Portugal and my determination to not spend a single euro that I didn't have to, we'd had limited opportunities to conspire. I called her some evenings but the last two or three times she'd been with Connor, and she always seemed like she couldn't wait for the call to end, or I'd hear him in the background trying to get her attention. So I just stopped ringing her. It made me unreasonably annoyed and a little bit jealous. Connor gave me bad vibes; a gut feeling I could never shake when I was near him. I hated that he was Charlie's best friend. He was always at the pub, in the car, on the sofa, at the door; just *there*, all the time, with his weird little comments towards me like *alright headbanger* or *your father is banned from my uncle's pub, did ya know that?* or *oh, I didn't know she was coming with us.* I was never anything but polite. I didn't want to fight with him, because I thought both Doireann and Charlie would pick him over me in a heartbeat. So I smiled, tried not to hate him, and worked instead on making sure everyone else loved me.

The last Saturday of August was twenty-seven degrees outside; practically Mediterranean. The sun was piercing, punishing. I could feel it irradiating my skin when I stood in it for more than a minute or two, could almost hear the outer layer of my body crisping, the light breaking down the vitamin D in my fat cells. That's how we get vitamin D from the sun, you know; it's literally cooking us alive. The sun is nothing but a giant oven filament, red-hot and basting us in our own juices. But inside was cool, breathy, the sheen of sweat on skin drying to nothing but a thin, uncomfortable layer of grime. It was almost a pleasure to go to work. Almost.

I was restocking the receipt roll in the till when I spotted him, head bowed slightly, left hand holding his glasses out at an angle from his small brown eyes so he could better read the writing on a packet of drill bits. *Reliable. Strong. Stands the test of time. Secure anything.* The back of his neck had a dirty tan and his t-shirt hung crookedly on his top-heaviness. His hair was still cropped close to his skull, his unruly beard running into it, the whole lot peppered with grey. A sun-aged tattoo stuck out from the bottom of his t-shirt cuff; a raised fist in front of a tricolour. I dropped the receipt paper and it bandied to a halt under the counter, unrolled and now probably unusable. My father turned and so did I; I stood, back to him, facing Nadia who had already started to scold me.

—Jesus, butterfingers... are you okay? You're a funny colour.

I gave my head a little shake. I could hear his boots approaching the counter.

—I feel sick. Can I get some air?

—Yeah. I have Rennies in my cubby if you want some.

I unlatched the counter and scooted under it, letting it fall closed with a slap as I darted into the aisles and out the door. I didn't stop to check if he'd seen me too. Even if he had, would he know me now? The last time he'd seen me, I was freshly eighteen and ready to leave town. He took me for a pint in

Gilligan's, the only pub that he wasn't barred from. He clapped me on the back and told me I was the best thing he'd ever done in his life. By midnight his head was lying on the bar and the bouncers grabbed him under the arms and deposited him on the footpath outside. It had been cold; I slung his battered, brown leather jacket over his shoulders and ordered a taxi. He wasn't fit to walk to the rank. When we got to his apartment I asked the taxi man to wait, handed him a fifty-euro note from Dad's wallet, and escorted my father in, putting him on the sofa on his side, taking off his boots, pouring him a pint glass of water and nabbing two Panadol from the kitchen cabinets. These I left on the coffee table beside him before throwing a blanket across his stretched-out, limp frame. I whispered goodnight and as I turned to leave he grabbed my hand and said *I love you, baby girl.* The words pinched me. The taxi was still there when I left. He drove me back to Hill Lodge and when he tried to hand me the change of the fifty I told him to keep it. Then I sat on the swing set and stared up at the cosmos until the clouds folded in and it started to rain, thought about all the times my father had told me he loved me that I could remember; on the morning of my Communion; out the window of his car when Máire kicked him out for the last time; standing next to my grandmother's embalmed, wizened body in the coffin. I tried to figure out why this one hurt the most as I searched the black velvet of the sky with eyes that were bloodshot and shining. I didn't hear from him again until Christmas; he called me on Stephen's Day and I could nearly smell the drink through the phone. Not even a card. Not even a call on actual Christmas. Just a drunken afterthought. Just like my existence.

Dad rang me exactly five times in the years I'd been in London. Twice to tell me of dead relatives, twice because he was drunk and decided he missed me, and once because he couldn't remember the exact address of our old house for some form thing he had to fill out. He wasn't an alcoholic in the traditional sense; he didn't wake up every morning and rinse his mouth with whiskey, didn't carry a hip flask, didn't take bottles of grog with him to his job as a landscaper, a job that he was actually incredible at. In fact, he could go weeks and weeks without so much as a drop. Then a random Friday would roll around and he'd get the thirst and nobody would see him again until Monday. My mother, barely twenty when she had me and resistant to the reality of motherhood, was also fond of a three-day bender. But eventually the fun wore off and the responsibility of having an actual child kicked in. She grew out of it. He grew into it. It seemed a particularly cruel pattern to me; just as soon as everything would settle down in our house, when he and my mother would be kissing each other in the doorways and singing together in the car and taking turns helping me with homework or books or tying my shoelaces, the inevitable Bad Friday would roll around, he'd take the week's wages with him and a big, fat, dark cloud would descend on my mother's head. His mobile phone would always be turned off. Once, we had no groceries in the house because he'd taken the money for the shopping, and she'd bundled me into the back of the car and driven the length and breadth of the town looking for him, weaving in and out of pubs with a jittery, wild aura about her, until finally I spotted him stumbling out of the same pub he'd take me for a pint in eleven years later, his arm slung

105

over the shoulders of a slim woman with a tight green dress on. Máire flew across the road like a banshee and started showering him with weak blows of her fists; he grabbed her arms and pushed her into the wall of the pub. She fell to the ground like a jacket slipping off the back of a chair, and the woman laughed at her and flicked her cigarette ash at her before they kept walking. She spent a week in bed after that; not before borrowing a hundred euros off my grandmother for food, all things I could make on my own, porridge and bananas and noodles and bread and ham for sandwiches. She called my school and told them I had strep throat, so nobody missed me. The lie made me feel sick to think about because it meant I'd have to keep lying when I went back to school the following week. She locked the doors with the deadbolts and Dad spent what felt to me like hours pounding on every window of the bungalow, including my own, speaking to me coaxingly through the double-glaze, begging me to let him in. I so desperately wanted to. But I didn't want to make my mother feel worse, didn't want to hear them scream and swear until the sun came up. So I went and slept in the bath instead, wrapped up in a Winnie the Pooh sleeping bag, my pillow under my head, the cold porcelain turning sticky and warm under me. He was gone when I woke up. Every morning that week, I got up, made Máire tea and both of us toast, left hers on the locker beside her bed, where her small, skinny frame was curled up, an ouroboros, depression causing her to consume herself. She smelled bad, like an old gym bag, and her hair was a bird's nest, and I tried running her a bath but the water was cold because she wasn't lighting the fire in the mornings. I was cold too; I dragged my electric blanket off the bed and sat on the sofa all day watching TV, Jeremy Kyle and Ricki Lake and Dr Phil and Oprah soothing my anxieties, reducing the amount of time I spent biting my nails down to the quick. I was eight years old. I wished I had a big sister. I made one up for myself, Sabrina, the best big sister ever, and for a while that helped, but my ability to create convincing imaginary friends was waning by the day. I could feel the magic of it seeping out of my raw, bloodied nail beds. By the end of that week, Dad had come knocking, petrol station bouquet and box of off-brand Turkish Delight in hand, and Máire let him back in, and we resumed some semblance of a normal life until the next abscursion.

I hid around the side of the building until I saw him leave, his head bent against the sun, a box of drill bits and a new rake in his hands. He got into his work van, dirty and white, *Maher and Sons Landscapers* written on the side. He had no sons, just me, but he thought a family-oriented business name would get him more work. He did hire young lads during the summer holidays who could have been mistaken for his sons, probably for that very reason. I could feel perspiration growing on the back of my neck, running down under the collar of my polo shirt. *Why am I hiding? What harm could it do to say hello?* I considered crossing the car park, knocking on the window of the van. I'm sure he would have been happy to see me. So why did the thought of it make me feel so terrible? Eventually he drove off, and I slid back inside the shop, running a shaky hand through my damp hair. I worked the rest of my shift with a pain behind my eyes.

I wasn't happy. Every new day I had to live in this in-between place, stuck, I was even less happy. Happiness became a pale imitation, something I was able to slide on and off my face as the situation called for it. When Lily showed me her *Champion Speller* sticker, I hugged her and beauty-queen beamed, forcing the corners of my mouth up towards my eyes. When Máire bought me new pyjamas apparently for no reason other than to treat me, I smeared on a look of delight as I rubbed my fingers across the dyed cotton of the sleeve. When Charlie told bad joke after stoned bad joke, I laughed until my face ached from the effort. He was the only one I didn't always have to be *on* for, but even with him, the work I was putting into appearing normal was starting to mar the time we spent together. *Fake it 'til you make it.* Faking it was making me actively worse.

I was meant to take a taxi home. Instead, I gathered up my hoodie and bag, rolled a cigarette, and started walking. As I walked, I put my headphones in, put on Elliot Smith, and cried. I cried until I couldn't see and the sun was stinging my ruddy, sodden cheeks, eyes red raw and snot running out of me, wailing as I pounded the footpaths towards home, which was a hefty trek, but I didn't care. I just wanted to scream and cry and be alone and let all the misery run out of me onto the concrete of what happened to be the most affluent part of town. Us commoners called it Millionaire's Lane because all the houses were hulking Celtic Tiger monstrosities with ridiculous add-ons like half-scale tennis courts, outdoor pools, and three-car garages. I got a lot of looks out of car windows, nosy people on their way home from comfortable office jobs, slowing their eerily quiet electric cars down a bit to take a good look at me like they'd have to recount the shape of my face and my unhinged demeanour to a

Garda later on in the week when I was inevitably arrested for murder or arson or something. What was so bad about walking and crying? People did it all over the world every day. I wasn't hurting anyone. I did want to rip my own skin off but wanting to hurt someone doesn't count as malicious when it's only yourself.

After an hour, my feet were burning in my work runners, rubbing blisters into my pinky toes, my heels, the balls of my feet. So I took them off and carried them, purple socks blackening on the footpath, which was waning, turning into cracked, melty tar and white line the further out of town I walked. The higher and thicker the hedgerow got, the safer I felt, and about twenty minutes from home I had stopped crying. My mouth was dry and my eyes itched. I sat into the ditch and rolled another smoke and drank the last of a warm, flat bottle of Diet Coke that had been bouncing around in my handbag for about three days. It coated my teeth unpleasantly, made my tongue feel thick and furry. Cigarette smoke should never be a preferred taste. I was tired, so very tired. Dog-tired. Heartbroken-tired. The grass underneath my arse was cool and a bit damp and I laid back in it, dragging myself in a little closer to the dandelion and honeysuckle and thistle, a little further away from the smell of the warm tarmac. Next to me lay a curious patch of bare earth, bladeless, leafless, like it had been poisoned or dug up or scorched. Creeping nettles and thorny spindly bramble encircled it, like the earth was trying to protect itself from any more human interference, keep itself safe until it healed again. If I were a more ambitious person, I might have dug up the soil with my hands to see if anything was buried there.

My father's face swam back into my mind's eye, my own face really, the two interchangeable and yet incongruous.

The road my mother and her family lived on was isolated. Maybe two or three cars would pass in a full hour. I was more or less left alone in the ditch. I thought about telling Máire I'd seen Dad today and immediately decided against it. No, she wouldn't have any words of comfort for me, no soothing aphorisms or even a gentle pat on the hand. She'd just say something like *you're wasting your time even thinking about him* and then I'd feel even worse. I could hear bees in the hedgerow, a low and slightly sinister hum leaking from the greenery. I'd never been stung by a bee. I could have been deathly allergic and I wouldn't have had a notion. A wisp of temptation crossed my brow. Before I could act on it, a car pulled up. Charlie's head popped out the rolled-down window. I sat up.

—Christ, I thought you were dead. What are you doing, you lunatic?

—Got a bit tired on the walk home.

He looked at me oddly before telling me to get in the car. I was puce, embarrassed at having been caught being undeniably weird by the one person I wanted very much to think I was *not* weird; I tried to play it off as I got into the car, like *haha aren't I so cool, so quirky?* But it doesn't really matter what your worldview is; lying in the ditch next to the road is not a cool or quirky thing to do. It's concerning at best.

—You coulda called me for a lift, y'know.

—I was enjoying the walk, to be honest.

—You heading home?

—Unfortunately, yes.

He took his eyes off the road to look at me, and I blushed again, and instead of pulling into my mother's driveway, he kept going, past her house, and down to the end of the road where he turned right for the lake. He reached over and grabbed my hand, briefly squeezing, and the heat of my face met my hairline.

—Open up the glove compartment there and roll a joint.

—You keep weed in the car? Are ya not afraid you'll be pulled?

—Nah. Hasn't happened yet anyway. Don't jinx it.

I rolled, and crumbly little bits of weed littered the fabric of my leggings as he took bend after twisty bend, crossing the bump of a bridge, the shore coming into view. The sun hung low now, gestational, resting on the barely rippling water. He stopped the car and we got out. I still had no shoes on. I took my socks off too; they were filthy and embarrassing now so I quickly balled them up and shoved them into the bottom of my handbag.

—Just wanna feel the grass on my feet. I think they call it grounding.

—They do. Ma does it every morning on the lawn before she drinks a cup of herbal piss.

—Suppose I'd know that if I ever met her.

He looked at me strangely. I made it awkward. I lit the joint and we passed it back and forth as we walked the shore. The stretch of grass had little lumps of gravel and grit hidden in it and I winced occasionally. I'd have to soak my feet when I got home and standing on them tomorrow would be a nightmarish foray into podiatry torture.

—So what's wrong with you?

I blinked, stoned and shook to the core.

—Beg your pardon?

—No one lies in the ditch like a dead body unless they're going through some shit.

—Not true. I do it all the time. It's my only hobby actually.

—Fine, don't tell me.

I agonised; tell the truth or deflect? Be vulnerable or be a Cool Girl? I chewed my thumbnail, stared across the lake without really seeing anything.

—I'm just due my period. Makes me a bit insane, the week before.

Not the real truth, but not a lie either; just vulnerable enough. I did get a bit mad the week before. Once I cut my hair into a bob with blunt kitchen scissors and then sat on the floor crying, ruefully clutching the lengths I'd just cut off, and then my period came two days later and it all made sense.

III

September came and all of a sudden my mother's house grew deathly silent between the hours of 9 a.m. and 4 p.m., and although it meant I was no longer being used for free childcare on my days off, I wasn't too fond of being alone all day. I missed my sisters. I missed their questions and their screeches and their giggles and their bickering. I liked it when they came to me with things, liked that they saw me as somebody important, somebody with answers. I slept more; if I didn't have work, I wouldn't emerge from the room until after lunchtime unless I was going outside for a smoke. The festival was the second week of the month, and a big group of us were going. Two hundred euros to lie in my own tent in a cold, wet field twenty minutes from my mother's house seemed scandalous to me, but everyone I knew and liked was going and if I'd had to watch the whole thing on Instagram I would have been a real suicide risk, like a 'hide all the belts and sharp objects'-level threat. I wasn't having a good time. In fact, I was having a pretty terrible time, and if I was being truthful with myself, I'd been having a terrible time since I'd come home and maybe even before that. Some mornings, particularly on the days when I didn't have work, I'd sort of half-wake, keeping my eyes closed and my brain suspended in the cloudy liquid of sleep, and that was probably the happiest I could feel at any point because I couldn't latch onto any one concept. My thoughts were static, primal; *bed soft, skin warm, body safe*. I could slip into a pleasant dream with ease, generally ones about Granny Maher and her dogs, or being at the lake as a child, or being with Charlie anywhere at all, and I'd try to stay there long into the morning and towards the afternoon.

I'd taken to locking the bedroom door – the key was hidden on the top of the doorframe and I'd found it by chance one day, play-fighting with Gracie and Emilia, the heavy thuds of our footsteps shaking the top floor of the house and knocking the key down. Máire hadn't wanted me to have it, clearly, or she would have given it to me when I moved in. That night I locked the door for the first time and slept like a log. Máire loathed the thought of anyone sleeping longer than her in the mornings, couldn't bear the fact that I wouldn't be as miserable as her for the first forty minutes of my day. So if I wasn't up and about when she was, she'd come into the room, turn on the light, open the curtains, inform me of the time, and leave again. The first morning after I'd locked the door, I was already awake, just waiting to see what she'd do. She tried the handle, paused, tried to force the handle, and then left. Ten minutes later, the vacuum was going outside the door, the head of it being dragged loudly back and forth across the floorboards, and I lay in bed smiling at my victory, headphones in, listening to The Velvet Underground, imagining the rage coursing through her pedigree veins.

———

The whole drive out to the campsite, I was a raw nerve. The back seat was littered with Charlie's two-man tent, sleeping bags, camping chairs, my suitcase, and crates and crates of drink, not only ours but Connor's, Doireann's, and Seány's. We met Connor and Seány inside the gates of the car park. Connor was wearing a dashiki and a pair of John Lennon sunglasses. Already his nose was twitching. I had to stop myself from physically cringing. He was the worst. He and Doireann were still on and off; I'd outwardly been a supportive friend but my inner bitch yelled *dump him* every time she brought him up in conversation. They sat into the car, shoving all our camping stuff into an unceremonious pile in the centre so the poles of the tent were poking me in the ear. Connor tore open a box of Orchard Thieves and passed us a can each.

—We're set up across from the jetty. Jamie and his moth and a few of her mates are beside us. Fucking melters.

His next move was to reach into his sock and take out a bag of coke. He took a sizable bump before offering the bag around. I went last, dipping the acrylic tip of my pinky finger into the bag and scooping out a little pile. I asked Connor if I could take a second bump for luck. Charlie eyeballed me, said no thanks to the bag, said it was a bit early in the day for him, tightened a hand on the steering wheel even though the car was parked. I evened out my nostrils and twenty minutes later I could feel my pulse in my eyeballs. I slid on my sunglasses, vintage tortoiseshell ones with round, gradient lenses that I'd picked up at a flea market and that had fit my features so perfectly I was instantly sad because I knew that one day I'd lose them, break them, or forget about them somewhere, on the seat of a bus maybe, or the back of a toilet in a pub or something. That was a very *me* move. I kept St Anthony inundated with pleas for house keys, earrings, passports, and bank cards. We made moves, unpacking the car at speed. Bolder now, I hoisted out the tent and thrust it at Connor to carry.

The boys set the tents up while I sat and watched from a camo camping chair, my open can in the net pocket of the left arm. When Doireann arrived she was wearing a neon-yellow bra and a pair of black fishnets hiked up over tiny black shorts, her Doc Martens shiny, her tan perfect, her face glistening with little gems all stuck on carefully in the shape of a Mardi Gras mask. Next to her, I looked positively plain. I lacked the body confidence to bare my belly button, buried in between layers of puppy fat that I'd never managed to shift, and at the sight of her I tugged at the hem of my t-shirt, wrapped my arms around my own waist, made myself smaller. Connor dropped the poles of my tent and crossed to greet her, grabbing a fistful of her arse while tongue-kissing her; she both leaned back and then pitched forward, embarrassed but enjoying it all the same. I rolled my eyes and stopped myself from kicking him in the back of the knees.

—Oi, soft-jaws, put her down and pick up the end of these fucking poles before I impale you with them.

Charlie was standing, one hand on his hip, the other brandishing the half-assembled two-man tent. He looked so put out that I stifled a laugh. Connor ignored him so I stood to help, threading the flexible fibreglass through the nylon. Doireann and Connor were still wearing the faces off each other. Charlie looked disgusted.

—Let's agree to never be that sickening.

—Amen.

This agreement died with the first pill. At the main stage, we crashed together, teeth and limbs and lips and fingers disintegrating like matter inside a wormhole, stretched out, liquidated. His incisors against the skin of my neck made me shudder pleasantly, made my eyes roll back in my head like loose marbles. His hair looked sugary and soft under the purple light; I wanted to consume him and have him radiate out from between my ribs like a sacred heart. The ecstasy rolled from my stomach up into my mouth again and I let it take over me, beads of sweat peeling from my skin like fish scales, molars flattening a strip of chewing gum into flavourless nothingness, eyes darting behind the safe tint of my sunglasses. One wrong move and I could spin out like bald tyres on ice, spiralling, spitting nails, chewing on my lips until they split and bled. Charlie took my face in his warm, glorious hands, pushed up my glasses, and kissed me hard in time with the drop of the music. I felt all the knowledge of the universe pass between our mouths. When he pulled away he reached into my bum-bag and pulled out a cigarette, pressed his lighter to it in the middle of the crowd. Faint paranoia pulled at me but I just flipped my glasses back down, pushed a sheaf of my hair off my sticky neck, and took the smoke from him. If I stood totally still I'd implode so I just kept bobbing, kept chewing, kept kissing and dancing and laughing and glittering, a strung-out fairy under a disco-ball moon.

—You're so fucking beautiful.

Charlie was in my ear again. His voice sounded shuddering, glitchy, like ones and zeros on an ancient computer screen. My teeth threatened to split my face in half with the smile. I was a walking cliché on this one, but no man had ever called me beautiful before without me, rather pathetically, asking for it. I was at the peak of my high and I was sure no words would ever sound so glorious to me ever again, except the three that had begun to swim around my fishbowl skull like neon tetras, glowing: *I love you.*

The comedown was a nightmare.

After what seemed like millennia, we slept, spooning in the humid little two-man tent, the sun already breaking through the line of trees to the east of the campsite. I spent the better part of two hours crying silently, my head aching, my heart in my stomach, wishing to God I'd just stayed home in my mother's house and watched another ancient film in the cool, dark confines of the spare room. My sleep was broken and useless. When I woke up, I immediately hauled myself out of my sleeping bag and hung out the unzipped door of the tent to puke a river of cider-vomit and melancholy, and the people camping beside us, already up and drinking cans, scrunched up their faces and said *Jeeeesus*, but I didn't have it in me to care. The light made my eyes itch and water so I put my trusty sunglasses back on, squeezed my lids shut, and searched around in my overnight bag for two ibuprofen and the Xanax I'd stolen from Máire. Water in my mouth was a revelation. I swished away all the grit and silt of the night before, spat it out, and took the pills before lying back down next to Charlie, who hadn't so much as snored at all my noise. I tried to sleep again, but my brain was full of static, and I could feel the second, filthy skin of makeup pasted to my face. I would have sold my left leg for a cup of tea. So I gave up on sleep and found my face wipes, scrubbing the glittery crust of the night from my eyes and cheeks and chest, trying for all the world to resemble only half a scumbag, before pulling on Charlie's hoodie over my bra and setting off in search of something that would heal me.

The campgrounds were awash with quiet despair. I was not the only half-dressed cretin in shades shuffling like the living dead, and as I joined the end of the queue for the coffee van I felt tears gather in the corners of my sandy eyeballs. A stranger in front of me offered me a toke of his joint and I took it, and the minute I handed it back I started to panic about cold sores and scabies and gingivitis. I couldn't swallow. Instead, I let my potentially diseased spit just sit under my tongue, gathering viscosity, harbouring deadly germs. When it was my turn to order I got a cup of scalding water alongside my tea and Charlie's oat milk latte, and the whole walk back to the tent resisted the urge to throw it in my own face. When I put the cups down I spat once more, discreetly, into a tissue, then swished the hot water, feeling it pucker and singe my taste buds, burning away the badness. That was better. I used the last of the water to try to wash away my puke from earlier, pulled out my camp chair, sat back, and prayed over my tea, trying to make it holy water. Charlie's curly head appeared through the tent zip, his face just as drawn and pale as mine.

—Good fuck. Were we thumping the shite out of each other all morning or what?

—Don't even talk to me. I feel like a bag of smashed testicles.

—That's… an interesting analogy.

—You so much as show me a pill later on and I'll karate kick it out of your hand.

He clambered out, pulled on a t-shirt, opened his own chair out, and sat next to me, taking the coffee cup from my limp hand. It was quiet as we smoked a cigarette; Connor and the others remained asleep, presumably, their tents closed up and silent, our circle void of everyone but us, empty cans, and a lone, battered sleeping bag. For that I was grateful. In my state, I'd only hate the sight of them.

—Why the fuck would we camp when we literally live twenty minutes from here?

—I literally thought the same thing when I woke up. We're absolute dopes.

—I'll drive you to mine for a shower in a bit if you want. We could get a takeaway then, get fresh and come back.

—If God exists, he sent you to me.

—Yeah. Nice hoodie.

I smiled for the first time that day, sheepishly, and he reached out his hand and put it on my leg. It stayed there until Connor emerged from his camo-print two-man with a can of Prazsky, whereupon Charlie quietly took it back and folded his arm across his stomach.

We drove to Charlie's house after eleven; my stomach was in knots, getting worse the closer we came to the two-storey pebbledash monstrosity he called home. His parents were posh, horsey types who had once been able to put their children into expensive, refined extracurriculars like piano and ballet and rugby and showjumping, college funds open since conception, the best of everything made available to them once they knew the merits of hard work – which, in this case, consisted of mucking out horse sheds and wheel-barrowing fresh hay and washing the jeep with the hose and a cloth. The recession had shaken them, he told me; they got to keep the house but the horses were a thing of the past, with only his mother's favourite remaining in the paddock for regular riding, the stalls in the yard behind the house empty of broodmares. Now, his father worked in the stone quarry with JJ three miles away, and his mother taught small children riding lessons in the Lakeland Stables Equestrian School. When he started his mechanic apprenticeship, they paid for it on the proviso that when he was qualified, he'd reimburse them for room and board. He worked out of their garage now, mostly on bikes and bangers belonging to his friends and the general scraw of young men dotted around the area, but he gave his parents a cut of every sale. And he didn't even seem sore about it. I was hoping to God for the third time that day. *Please don't let them be home.* Charlie promised they wouldn't be; his little sister had an Irish dancing feis in Sligo so they were supposed to be gone for the day, and to my intense relief the yard was empty.

The inside of the house was a shock after waking up in a field. The kitchen was a dream of virgin marble and rosy brass fittings, glass cabinets and smooth, polished surfaces cleaned to the point of reflection. They had a dresser full of unsettling, expensive-looking horse figurines and crystal glasses with long, flawless stems. I envisioned wholesome family dinners and Christmas mornings spent together, sporting matching jumpers and Colgate smiles.

—Cup of tea?

—Yeah, please.

I stood with my feet glued together and my hands clasped at my abdomen, chewing the dead skin off my bottom lip. My mother would have pried my shoes off at the door and hosed me down before letting me inside. She definitely wouldn't have even considered letting Charlie past the door with oil-slick hands blackened from tinkering with bike parts. Charlie put the kettle on to boil and led me into the sitting room. I took my shoes off before hitting carpet, my runners dusty with dried muck from the night before. He handed me two remote controls.

—Here, stick on a film or something and I'll be back. *Mi casa es tu casa.*

The Spanish sounded queer in his flat Midlands accent, both butchered and lyrical. I nodded and watched him leave, feeling dwarfed by the magnitude of the house, my hangover and anxiety causing my temperature to spike, my hands slick. I looked at the remote controls and the buttons seemed melded together, soupy and hard to identify. My palms were turning the backs of the controls damp. I placed them on the coffee table, an abstract lump of dark oak smoothened, levelled, and varnished to fit in with the other furniture, a gargantuan suede sofa and various side tables sporting lamps, books, coasters. The weird pocks and divots of death still marked the underbelly of the table. I ran a finger along the underneath, the grooves solid under my touch.

Charlie's mother had an entire back wall devoted to family photos. I approached it slowly, edging around the sofa, eyes and hands and ears and mouths coming into focus as I stepped closer, socks rough on cream shag. Dozens of facsimiles of Charlie and his family stared out at me, occupying living rooms, community halls, winner's podiums, and back gardens, all part of one huge, blinding mosaic. There were school sports days, Communions, graduations, showjumping action shots, debs dates, fiftieth birthday parties, expressions of joy, concentration, excitement, teenage resentment. I wanted to step into each one for a minute or two and leave a little bit of me behind; a fingernail, a sock, some strands of hair. I turned and sat down on the floor next to the sofa, my back pressed against the stuffed, comfortable base, and fiddled with the remote controls again.

The Saturday evening, it was a little harder to get into the mood. As Doireann sat cross-legged in front of me sticking pink gems to my face with eyelash glue, I felt like my heart was going to explode with anxiety. The tent was uncomfortably close even though we had the front flap wide open, held back with a big hair-clip because the ties were gone missing. I told Doireann about my tachycardic episode and she paused, tweezers hovering near my right eye.

—That's just the hangover. Drink through it, don't be a soft touch.

She was right. She sat back so I could take a swig of wine from the bottle we were sharing. It was pink and disgusting, but it cost a fiver and we couldn't afford to be choosy.

—Make me look like a ride. I haven't the capacity to be verbally charming today.

—You're always a ride. But I have to say, I'm working magic here.

—Speaking of. Any white left?

She shot me a look.

—Ah go on. Charlie's bringing mine later on.

Charlie and Connor were gone to pick up party favours for everyone. She was still looking at me. I did a little puppy-dog face; two gems popped off my forehead and fell onto my lap. She tutted as she picked them off my thigh.

—Right. But don't be a little fucking Henry the Hoover. You handed me back a licked baggie the last time.

—You're the bestest.

As she pulled my hair into two buns she told me she'd called things off with Connor that morning.

—Sure he was snapping other girls the whole time, hiding the phone when we went to bed and all so I wouldn't look through it. You know Erin Kelly? She sent me screenshots of him this morning with the mickey out trying to get her to send him nudes back. You're lucky yous were gone before I started on him.

—That is manky behaviour on his part.

—Yeah, tell me about it. We were never official anyway. So we said we were gonna stay mates cause like I do like him as a person but like if he's just gonna keep lying to me then we're better off as friends.

I nodded along thoughtfully. I personally wouldn't have given him the steam off my piss if he was dying of thirst, but that wasn't my choice to make.

By the time Connor and Charlie showed up again we were well on it; I was so cokey I needed to keep my sunglasses on even though the sun had receded behind a bank of cloud hours before. Doireann was the same. She was talking at the top of her lungs and I was laughing maniacally at all of her funny stories. The other people in our little encampment were obviously growing bored of us, but that's because they were anti-craic. Connor was right about that. A pack of fucking melts. Charlie slipped a hand into the back pocket of my shorts, kissed me on the hair surreptitiously.

—Well hello gorgeous. Very… sparkly.

—Not so bad yourself. Where were ye?

—Ended up stuck talking to a lock of lads from school. You know yourself, one minute it's hello and the next you're caught listening to a ream of shite about someone's smelly kids and their shitehole job.

Something about his tone of voice made me feel funny. Or maybe it was the way he turned his face away from me when he said it. But I knew I had just been lied to. I didn't say anything; my mouth was suddenly dry, my heart jumping up and down my throat like a rubber ball on a hardwood floor. I wanted to rip his hand out of my pocket. I took three deep breaths and convinced myself I could smell perfume that wasn't mine or Doireann's. *It must be off him then. Whose fucking perfume is that?* I tried to see out of the side of my sunglasses, eye him over, check for hickeys or makeup-smudges, something tell-tale. But then he moved away from me and took out his phone and started texting. *Who's he texting? Sure all his friends are literally right here.* I listened, ears piqued with all the sonic concentration of a fox on the hunt; Connor's phone dinged seconds later. He pulled it out, read the message, looked at Charlie with a grin, and nodded slightly. I didn't imagine that. Maybe the perfume was phantom but that definitely happened. I decided to test the waters.

—Everything alright?

—Yeah. Come on, we neck a can and head to the arena.

—You smell funny.

—What?

—You smell like perfume or something.

He leaned back from me just enough that I noticed, rubbing his neck until it turned pink under his fingers.

—It's probably yours.

It definitely, *definitely* wasn't mine. I was wearing Vanilla Musk body spray that I'd robbed off Doireann. My stomach was writhing, unable to digest the lie on top of the lie. I rooted the rest of the wine out of the tent and drank a mouthful, the taste cheap and burning, seething enough to snap me out of my spiral.

—Can I get that half gram off ya?

—Haven't picked it up yet. I've to meet them on the way up, at the gate to the other campsite. Posh cunts are in the yurts.

Now I was angry as well as anxious. *Where the fuck were they if they weren't getting the bags?* Why did he say *them* and not *him*? I drank more wine; I actually emptied the bottle and threw it back into the tent, forcing down the urge to projectile vomit, composing myself, pushing my sunglasses back into place.

—Right. Get them into ye and let's go.

I turned my back to Charlie and held out a hand to Doireann, pulling her up from her camp chair. We linked arms and started running towards the arena, giggling like mad, faster and faster, my legs like electrified elastic bounding over tufts of grass and outstretched legs and emptied flagons of cider, lit joints and portable speakers, pizza boxes and girls in denim shorts, running until I couldn't breathe and Doireann was tugging on my arm to slow down before she collapsed, and when we turned to look back Charlie and Connor and everyone else were Barbie-sized on the horizon, still weaving through the tents and the people.

—Are – you – okay?

Doireann was panting, hands on her knees, her words breathy and full of effort.

—Not really, but sure fuck it.

—Did he say something to ya? I'll fight him.

—No, nothing like that. Just a feeling. Ja ever just get a feeling?

—Women's intuition. Don't doubt it.

—Yeah.

Inside the arena was already a sea of sticky, glimmering bodies; different music pumped from different speakers and all of it managed to converge in the centre, a raucous, almost intolerable mess of sound. We moved from bar to bar and stage to stage, always a drink in both hands. Doireann and I decided that instead of queueing for a manky green Portaloo to do our drugs, we'd just cover each other as we took keys, ducking down into her handbag in a big group of people as if we were looking for something inside, sniffing as quickly as possible and then straightening back up. We had to be clever about it. We couldn't go directly after one another. One of us would take her turn and then we'd weave and bob in through a different throng of people and the other one would have a go. I hadn't seen Charlie since I'd turned my back but that didn't stop my every thought centring itself on him. *Where is he now? Why hasn't he tried to ring my phone?* I shouted to Doireann over the din, her hands above her head, her hips bopping from one side to the other.

—Has Connor tried to ring you at all?

—Nah. Bit of a relief, really.

We were in the EDM tent and she had her eyes on a lad with about fifteen glowsticks hanging around his neck in big, rigid, neon circles. He kept trying to dance up near us and I kept moving us back until we were against the metal railings, too anxious to deal with the presence of a strange man. I closed my eyes to everything. The stupid rhythmic breathing wasn't working anymore. I drank; I drained both my plastic cups of their sickly mixed alcohol and waited for it to slow me down so I could take more coke. When I opened my eyes again Doireann was attached to glowstick man at the mouth. It looked like they might inhale each other. I closed my eyes again. I moved my body to a beat I didn't care about. I felt more alone in an arena black with people than I'd felt in a while. I was drowning in the solitude. I took another bump. It brought me back up. I tried to call Charlie but he didn't answer. Doireann's coke was nearly gone. I had to find him before she got annoyed with me. She was still shifting the glowstick man. I texted her that I was going to the bar and weaved my way back out to the thoroughfare, looking for Charlie. I thought I'd have to look for ages; I found him within ten minutes, him and Connor and Doireann's friend Kelsey. She was laughing hard at something Charlie had said, her crossed legs angled towards him, a hand placed strategically near his on the bench. I hated her on a metaphysical level. I wanted to grab her by the hair and rip her backwards off the bench and into the fucking dirt. I inserted myself into the conversation.

—Heya!

I dropped down and kissed Charlie on the cheek before sidling in next to him; Kelsey stared at me. I stared right back. *That's right, bitch. Mine.*

—Where did you come out of?

—EDM tent. Do ya ever check your phone?

—Sorry, I was chatting.

—Did ya get that yet?

He slid a balled-up fist over my lap and dropped the little Ziploc bag onto the fabric of my shorts. Then he turned right back to his conversation with Kelsey. Anger and something else, something more dangerous, shot through me. My heart was flying; I could have reached down into my throat and pulled it out. Connor was giving me little dirty sly looks out of the corner of his eye and frantically texting on his phone. Looking for Doireann now, I bet, because there was nobody to make sure she wasn't with another man. I didn't care. He wasn't worth her. He'd never ask me where she was because I'd have the power in that situation. I knew how people like Connor worked. I'd known them all my life. I could smell the badness off them even when everyone else couldn't. I leaned over to pick up someone's Clipper to light my rollie and I smelled the perfume again, stronger. It was Kelsey.

—Wow, that perfume is lovely. What is it?

Charlie shot me a look like *please don't.*

—Oh, thanks. It's Mugler.

—Well it's really fucking nice. Isn't it, Charlie?

—Eh, yeah, it's nice I guess.

My hands were shaking. The chat died. I created a big bubble of tension that enveloped the whole picnic bench.

Eventually Kelsey stood up. She put a hand on Charlie's shoulder, her pink acrylics gently pressing into his flesh as she squeezed it.

—I think it's best if I head off. Give me a shout later. And if ye see Doireann tell her I'm looking for her. Kiss kiss.

I'd rather have choked on my own vomit than told Doireann Kelsey was looking for her. She sauntered off, wearing her stupid self-satisfied smile, and I sneered back at her, lightning in my eyes. Charlie was staring at his phone, leaning on one hand, all of his body language screaming *leave me alone*. I didn't understand. I didn't get it. Why was he being like this? Why couldn't he want me all of the time instead of Monday to Friday? Worst of all, why couldn't I just fucking ask him?

—What? Something I said?

—I dunno. She's my friend.

—Yeah, okay. And I'm the Pope.

He was staring down at his phone again, clearly not going to give me the reaction I needed. I began to grind my teeth to dust in my mouth to relieve some of the tension my entire body seemed entombed in. By the grace of God, Doireann stumbled over. I stood up and embraced her like she'd just come back from war and I thought I'd never see her again. I kissed her on the cheek and she laughed a gorgeous, musical laugh, a laugh that dripped with self-esteem.

—Where were you?

Connor's voice was pissy. He had the tip of his hoodie string between his teeth.

—With some of the girls from school. We were having a bop.

I said nothing.

—Do you think I'm slow?

—What?

—Did the girls from school smear your lipstick all over your chin?

—Go fuck yourself.

—You're such a whore.

—That's rich coming from you, Mister I-send-pictures-of-my-tiny-dick-to-everyone.

—Shut your fucking drunk mouth, ya tramp.

That was it for me.

—Shut the fuck up, Connor, and go and blow your nose, ya quivering little troglodyte bastard.

—Ooh, big words from a big mouth. None of your business.

—A face not even a mother could love.

—Lads, don't be kicking off.

Charlie was standing now, hands outreached, trying to restore peace. People were staring. Connor jumped up, back straight, ran a hand across his nostrils, took off his hat, like he was going to fight Charlie. Nobody moved for a few agonising seconds. Then Connor put his hat back on and started to walk off.

—Well? Are you gonna come with me or not?

Charlie looked at me like he was in pain.

—I'll come find you later on.

Then he took off after Connor. They left us sitting at the damp wooden picnic table, both apoplectic with rage.

—Hey, fuck this.

I shook the little bag of coke at Doireann and gestured

back into the fray. Why should men be the only ones allowed to be aloof and debauched and free?

At the main stage, Doireann and I threw back our heads and screamed lyrics like they were the only words we had left to say. I shouted so hard I could feel blood forming in beadlets inside my throat, taste the metal on the back of my tongue. And then suddenly I really couldn't breathe. And then I couldn't see, or stand, and one hand was clutching my neck while the other patted my chest, like *help me fucking help me before I have a heart attack fucking Christ I can't die here, not here in the dirt and the sorrow of the fucking Midlands, I won't die that way, I won't I won't I won't.* Doireann hauled me to the back, away from the crowd, and then there was a steward in a hi-vis vest on either side of me. They took me to the medical tent and sat me on a gurney and I kept trying to gulp in air, like a fish pulled out of a tank, my mouth gaped and gasped and suffocated me worse, and Doireann was telling the medic what I had taken tonight, and where we were when it happened, and he says it doesn't sound like an overdose. He said it sounds like a panic attack. I was sitting there unable to fucking breathe and this useless Order of Malta bastard said I was having a panic attack. I wanted to see a real doctor. A volunteer steward was standing next to me, patting my knee sympathetically, telling me to look into her eyes and try to slow my breaths down. I knew what a panic attack was and this felt a thousand times worse. But then I thought about it, and somewhere inside of me I knew he was right, and that jolt of self-awareness alone was enough to bring my breathing down a bit, and then a minute later I got it under control another bit, and Doireann handed me a bottle of water, and I sipped it, and after what felt like a thousand breaths taken in a little slower every time, I was breathing normally. My heart was still thundering, but it had stopped physically hurting. The medic listened to my chest, pressing his freezing stethoscope to my sticky, glittery skin. He pursed his lips and told me to go home and sleep it off. No need. I had sobered up dramatically. I asked for a sick bag and puked up something that smelled like a distillery. I handed it to a wide-eyed Doireann. She looked like she was afraid to touch me, afraid to set me off again.

—I'm okay.

The words came out shaky. I tried to stand and she clutched my sick bag to her with one hand and reached out with the other, as if to push me gently back down, before she thought better of it.

—I'm gonna go back to the tent.

—Are ya not gonna go home?

—And let my mother see me like this? Not on your life.

—I'm not sure it's a good idea, Sersh.

—Are you gonna help me or not?

She linked me back, her arm tight now on mine, her chatter incessant, like sticking a plaster on a faultline. She put me into mine and Charlie's tent and laid me down and kissed me on the forehead and told me she loved me. To call her if I needed anything. As if I were her child. I knew where she was off to. It deeply annoyed me. Probably because it was exactly what I wanted to do. Instead, I stared at the shadows of other people dancing against the polyester of the tent wall, bursting with life, exuberant.

I didn't see Charlie again until after the sun rose. He climbed into our tent quietly and lay down beside me, on top of his sleeping bag, shoes still on, the smell of that perfume lingering. We weren't official, so I had no right. But I still felt like the breath was stolen from my lungs. He pulled me into his chest and stroked my hair and whispered, very, very quietly, *sorry*. I couldn't address any of it. I just kept faking sleep.

IV

The town looked its best on Christmas Eve. The County Council had sprung for a new set of lights for Main Street, flashing stars and neon bells and a sign that said *Nollaig Shona*, and the pubs were full of merriment, people spilling out onto the footpaths in ugly jumpers and Santa hats, singing the same handful of Christmas songs that they'd been singing for twenty years or more. It was snowing, lightly, but snowing all the same, and everything was freshly powdered, glistening, virginal. Charlie asked me to go for a pint in Gilligan's.

—What, like a date?

—Yeah, like a date.

I took four hours to get ready. I used my mother's hot rollers to curl my hair, the end result soft, romantic, like Hedy Lamarr. I opted for a red lip and a clean cat-eye flick. I wanted to seem beautiful and unattainable. I sparingly sprayed my good perfume behind my knees, in my elbow crooks, on my neck, my wrists. I put on a matching lingerie set, black lace of course, and a pair of thigh-high stockings. My dress was black and almost knee-length, velvet, some cleavage but not too much. I pulled on my nicest heels and a leather jacket and tried not to panic. He picked me up outside my mother's front door; he actually drove up to the house and waited for me knowing my family were inside. That was huge.

—I know him.

—No you don't.

—I do. I *do* know him. His mother runs the lessons at the riding stables.

—Máire, please don't.

—What? I'm only saying. He's very handsome.

My mother and my sisters were all standing at the living room window looking out at Charlie, who gave them an embarrassed little wave. Máire waved back.

—Tell him to tell his mother I said hello.

—I'll see you later. Don't wait up.

—You have to be back in time before Santy comes.

Gracie looked up at me very seriously.

—I'll be back before Santy comes. I promise.

—Good, because he won't come if everybody isn't in bed.

—I pinky promise.

I extended my pinky finger and she wrapped hers around it. And then I said goodbye to everyone and half-ran out to the car. Charlie waited until we were at the end of the road to kiss me. It was long and sweet and I had to check my lipstick afterwards.

—You look great.

—Thanks. I try.

We were nervous. I felt like a virgin again. He held my hand on the way into the pub and I was elated. He ordered my favourite drink for me at the bar. I was moony-eyed and stumbling. All I ever wanted was all of his attention, and I was getting it. We sat into a booth, heads leaning together, conspiratorial and cosy.

—I quite like you, you know.

—I quite like you too.

—Like, *like*-like?

—Like *like*-like.

—We're such doses.

—I know. It's great.

—I don't wanna be a dose with anyone else.

—Me either.

We were holding hands again. I could never get over how perfectly our palms fit together. I reluctantly let go when he had to go to the bathroom. I said I'd go out for a cigarette and he could meet me there. I covered our drinks with coasters and took off out the back, smoke hanging out of my mouth, begging for the touch of the lighter. As I took the first pull, I heard my name. It was my father.

—By God, is that my little daughter?

—Hiya, Dad.

He hugged me. He reeked of Guinness. His hair was neat though, and his clothes were clean and pressed. Maybe he was just enjoying the Christmas. So why did I have a knot in my gut? I kept an eye over his shoulder and prayed Charlie would get held up on his way out.

—When did you come back? Why didn't you call me? Boys, boys, this is my wee one, my pride and joy, my one and only. Will you have a pint? You'll have a pint on me, on me, go into the bar and get whatever you want and another for meself.

He pressed a twenty-euro note into my hand. His friends were all looking at me. I wanted to crawl into a hole in the ground. I went to the bar instead and did what he told me to do. I couldn't see Charlie so I texted him *meet me back at the table*. I returned to my father and gave him his pint. He swayed a bit when he took it from me.

—Ah thanks, love, keep the change, put that away into your pocket for a bag of chips later.

His nose was purple and veiny, his eyes bloodshot. His friends were looking at me again. I felt like I was going to explode out of my skin or collapse inwards like a dying star. I hated that I knew him this way. I wanted a father like JJ. I got a father like this instead, a father who couldn't think beyond himself, a father who couldn't be a father. I excused myself to the bathroom and returned to Charlie. It must have been written all over my face because he stood up and put his coat on. I necked the drink in my hand, and then the half-full drink I'd left beneath the coaster. No need for it to go to waste.

Out in the snow, waiting for a taxi at the rank, he asked me what happened.

—Ran into my shitty dad. Got reminded why he's a shitty dad.

—Do you want to talk about it?

—Not really.

And I didn't. I wanted to forget all about it. I pulled my jacket closer to me, flecks of snow melting on the top of my head, dripping onto my scalp, cold and tickly. Charlie took my chin in his hand and kissed me, long and slow. The world fell away. I wanted so badly to be his. I knew, somewhere inside the darkest, most unrelenting part of me, that I would never be.

On Christmas Day, if I'd had the choice I would've stayed in bed until dinnertime. Instead, at half four in the morning, my sisters crept into my room as quietly as they could, my door deliberately left unlocked just in case, shivering with the joy and anticipation of presents. They all three shook me awake and led me downstairs, telling each other to be quiet and skip the creaky stairsteps lest Máire shout us all back to bed. As they whisper-shouted to one another and tore sparkling wrapping paper from shiny Mattel boxes like hunters skinning rabbits, I made coffee and threw a shot of Baileys in, perched on the edge of the sofa arm while one after the other they offered up their presents to me for appreciation, and I murmured and cooed and raised my eyebrows and said things like *cool* and *wicked* and *can I have a go of that one?* When my coffee was gone I got up to make another, but Lily grabbed the drawstring of my dressing gown.

—Aren't you gonna open your ones?

She gestured to the seat of the armchair in the corner, on which sat a small heap of presents, perfectly wrapped in shiny white paper, silvery ribbons curled like pig's tails. I hadn't been expecting anything at all – the last time I was included in Santa presents was the year before I moved out, and every Christmas since then I got a bank transfer from my mother of one hundred and fifty euros with a note that said *happy xmas from all of us.* My father last sent a card when I was twenty. He sent it to my mother's address and it sat unopened until I came home to claim it. It was still unopened, sitting inside the top drawer of the bedside locker. I recoiled at the thought of reading it; it would only be picking a scab. I didn't tell my mother I'd run into him on Christmas Eve. She wouldn't have had anything helpful to say. She'd just drop a pearl like *what would you expect from a pig, only a grunt, Saoirse?*

Lily handed me the topmost gift, a small, slim parcel that I knew was a book before I unwrapped it. Inside was a copy of *Little Women*, and inscribed in the cover in my mother's hand was *My favourite. Maybe it can be yours too.* I turned my back to my sisters, fiddling with the wrapping paper, folding it up neatly, saving the ribbon for no reason. When I was stable, I opened the others. A hot chocolate gift set from Lily, Emilia, and Gracie with a pretty mug covered in delicate, hand-painted azalea petals of pink and purple. A new dressing gown. A pair of in-ear headphones with a noise-cancelling function. A hundred-euro voucher for New Look. A Charlotte Tilbury eyeshadow palette. A pair of Ralph Lauren Chelsea boots in my size. A stocking full of chocolate coins and chocolate Santas and chocolate reindeer lollipops. Máire was always very good at gift-giving. I'd gotten her a tri-fold silver locket from the jewellers her family had used for decades. I'd been paying it off since October. I'd put pictures of Lily, Emilia, and Gracie inside. I felt awkward at the thought of putting myself in. She cried when she opened it, thanked me, and said she'd snap a picture of me and Lily to put in so all of her babies could be next to her heart. She was three glasses of wine deep at that stage so I didn't put any stock in her words.

I helped her make dinner. It was just us, JJ, and the girls but still she cooked for forty people. It was rare to be with her and not want to peel my own face off after an hour. She still vexed me but I was more forgiving. When I was chopping the potatoes wrong, I let her correct me. When I laid the table, I said nothing as she came round behind me and rearranged the forks. I even let her lick her thumb and run it over my cheek to catch a stray fleck of something. She was just being herself, in her own house. Who was I to always have a problem with that? My sisters, tired from the excitement, their bellies full of rich food and selection box chocolate, were fussy and picking at each other by seven o'clock that evening. I had been keeping a steady buzz on since my morning Baileys coffee; their annoyed little voices and grabby hands were funny to me. They took everything so seriously. *No, that's my Barbie. Your one is over there, look, you already lost her shoes. No, I don't want to share my new Legos with you. Stop touching me with your gross feet. Mammy, she's on my side of the sofa. Mammy, she pulled my hair. Mammy, she's got a snot hanging from her nose and she won't blow it.* They never came to JJ to sort their squabbles. JJ was passed out on the sofa in the kitchen anyway, a paper crown slipping down over his eyes, turkey gravy splattered on his good Ben Sherman shirt. My mother's patience was wearing thin. Emilia asked her to fish Barbie's good pink stilettos out from behind the back of the coalbox in the living room and that was the last straw. Máire snapped and roared *if I have to get up from my chair one more time to deal with ye, everyone is going to bed and the Santy toys are getting given to the poor children.* Emilia cringed away from her voice, her little hands worrying the hem of her tartan dress, tears forming in her eyes. I ushered her into the living room and saved Barbie's heels, a little dirty with coal dust but I wiped them on my tights and they were good as new. My sisters were now deathly quiet, Máire's threat hanging over them like the sword of Damocles. I had to fix it. The disharmony was making me anxious, causing flashbacks to a childhood where nobody fixed things for me. They were just overtired little girls clamouring for attention like small children do. There was no need to shout. Even if my mother's threat had no credence, her tone of voice, the venom in it was threat enough.

I turned off the big light. I pulled the curtains. I made my sisters sit on the sofa, far enough apart that they couldn't keep annoying each other. I put a blanket on each of them. I found *Moana* on Disney+ and pressed play. I waited fifteen minutes and everyone was quiet. By then my mother was out the back sitting at the patio table, smoking her Vogues and drinking more wine. Her glass hadn't been empty all day. I sat next to her and bummed a smoke.

—This is my Christmas treat to myself. A box of cigarettes and a bit of peace and quiet.

—You don't have to justify yourself.

—I wasn't. Just making conversation.

—Oh. Sorry.

It was like we didn't know how to speak to one another outside of a crisis or an argument. I tried again.

—Thank you again for my bits. I've never read *Little Women* before.

—You'll love it. It's my favourite. Have you seen the film?

—Not yet.

—Me either. It's supposed to be very good. The wee Irish one is in it. Saoirse what's-her-face. Ronan.

I had no quarrel with Saoirse Ronan except that she had the same name as me and was far more talented and successful which made me automatically dislike her a bit. Another silence. Our plumes of smoke were strobed through with white light from the security light on the side of the house.

—Do you want to go in and watch it with me?

The girls were all asleep or close enough to it, heads lolling, dolls and books and selection boxes forgotten about. She took the sofa between Lily and Gracie, who laid her sleepy little head on Máire's lap, and I curled up in the armchair, cutting Moana off mid-note, and we passed a box of Milk Tray back and forth and watched *Little Women*, which seemed to negate the need for me to read the book but it was rare for Máire to want to do anything with me so I didn't want to say no. I was hooked instantly, rapt for the whole film, crying a little bit when Beth died, crying more at the end when Saoirse Ronan had her book printed, something about the triumph of a woman in that landscape moving me deeply. I turned back and Máire was as fast asleep as my sisters. I plodded out to the kitchen and shook JJ awake.

—Will ya give me a hand getting the girls up the stairs? They're all asleep.

He stood up slowly, the paper crown floating off his head and onto the floor. He carried the girls to bed one by one and said *I'll leave your mother to you*, which sent a bolt of panic through me, but I took a breath and gently jostled her awake.

—What?

—It's past midnight. You were asleep.

—Ah bollocks. Did I miss the film?

—You did. It's okay though.

—Sorry, pet.

Her voice was thick with sleep.

—It's okay.

—Fag before we go to bed?

I got up to go out the back and she pulled me back down to the sofa.

—We're going to be bold.

She pulled her Vogues and lighter out of her handbag and turned the lid of the box into an ashtray. It felt dangerous and forbidden to smoke in her lovely living room. I ashed my cigarette like a felon.

—Do you still read?

—Sometimes.

—You used to love reading. Remember the Christmas I got you all the Harry Potters? I don't think I heard a word out of you for a month.

—I do remember. I devoured them.

—Somewhere along the line you stopped asking for books as presents though.

—Probably because I was getting bullied for it.

—You weren't bullied. Were you?

—A bit, yeah.

The girls in my year in First Year actually used to take my fiction books out of my school bag and write mildly horrible stuff for me to find as I read along. *Saoirse is a fridget. Saoirse Maher loves Mr Cooney. Saoirse shifts books. Smiley face with tongue out.* It was kind of a creative way to fuck with me while still having plausible deniability. They'd also make indirect little jokes on social media about my lack of a chest, my bad fringe, and my imagined affair with Mr Cooney the

English teacher, who I obviously loved so much seeing as I loved reading and was good at English. Mr Cooney was in his sixties and bald as an egg. I started to get a knotty stomach when I tried to read so I stopped. I never told my mother. She had enough on her plate all the time and I didn't think I'd get sympathy; just an angry Máire pounding into the school and making everything worse. The other girls got bored of me soon enough anyway and moved onto the girl with a lazy eye and bad shoes. I never joined in, but I was relieved. The school year after that, I grew B-cups and started smoking fags in the handball alley and made friends with the same girls that bullied me. It made me feel power-ful, at the time. How can you be afraid of falling when you're already halfway down? I hadn't spoken to any of them since I moved to England and I preferred to keep it that way.

—No, you would have told me.

—It sorted itself out anyway. I'm fine now.

—You were getting shit and you never told me? Saoirse.

—It was fine, honestly. A bit of bullying does wonders for the character.

Máire went quiet. She looked horrified. I didn't think it was that big a deal.

I spent the morning of Stephen's Day getting ready to go to the pub. It was cold, sleeting; still, I layered tanning mousse into my pale, goosebump-flesh and stood with my arms out like a scarecrow for twenty minutes, shivering with the cold of the bedroom. The heating was on, but my radiator, unlike everyone else's in the house, only managed to run at a lukewarm sputter. I didn't want to say it to my mother or JJ so instead I put a hoodie on going to bed and toughed it out the rest of the time. The flat in London had only electric heaters on the walls and James told me to stop using them so much because I was running up the bill, even though I was the one who paid it. Prior to that, Hill Lodge was a damp hole of a place and we frequently couldn't afford the fuel for the back boiler. So I was used to bearing the sting of indoor cold. It did make my tan dry slower though. As I waited for it to dry, I balanced back and forth on the balls of my feet, stretching my hamstrings in preparation for eight hours of heel-wearing, and stared out the window at the sad smears of snow on the far hills, like rivulets of Styrofoam or dirty lamb's wool, a sorry display of winter washed out by the ever-present rain. I knew the tan was a waste of time. I knew the second I stepped out into the weather, I would have patches and streaks and turn the colour of old cheese hardening at the edges. Yet I persisted. As is the prerogative of every pale Irishwoman.

Doireann and I were meeting Charlie and Connor at Connor's house before we went to town. I already had my bottle of wine and was fighting the urge to break into it before its time. When my tan was dry I did my makeup, relishing the ritual of everything I was doing, carefully and deliberately massaging creams and powders into my face, turning myself into someone else, someone I liked the look of. I gave myself new eyes, two daggers of ice set into thick beds of faux mink. I drew myself a smile the colour of blood. I hid diamonds under my skin. I felt the power of it all culminating in my fingertips as they patted and picked and stroked, making something magic out of something painfully ordinary. I didn't like my bare face. It was roundly shaped and asymmetrical; one eye squinted more than the other, one nostril flared less, one eyebrow sat higher. Like two different faces split in half and spliced together. I'd also begun to sport a permanent pair of dark, purplish rings beneath my eyes, a consequence of something I hadn't identified yet. Makeup allowed me to change all of that, even if it was only temporary; a glamour that had to be removed before witching hour. When it was done, I very gingerly pulled my dress on over my head, holding the neck out at an angle so as not to smudge anything. I examined myself in the mirror, pulled the fabric away from my stomach to loosen it so I couldn't see the round hump of my abdomen through the velvet. I looked good enough. I'd look even better after a drink or three.

JJ, Máire, and the girls were going to his mother's house for Stephen's Day dinner, but beforehand they were visiting Concepta in the home. My aunt had taken her in for Christmas dinner and dropped her back that evening, a testament to Concepta's sour and grating nature, which not even the guilt of abandonment could outweigh. The dementia definitely made it worse, cutting the filter out from between her brain and mouth altogether. Máire asked me if I wanted to come, and when I said no she flinched like I'd thrown something at her but said nothing. She didn't speak to me for the rest of the morning, angry with me but unable to blame me; she wouldn't have gone either, given the choice. Our Christmas amnesty was waning, the coolness edging back into her demeanour when she had to interact with me, the irritation prickling beneath my skin when I had to reply. When they left, the house fell into an uncanny, twinkling silence. Máire had gone all out with the decorations and left the fairy lights on all day and night, their little yellowish flecks of light dancing on the stair banisters, the outside eaves, the kitchen windowsill, the giant fake fir tree in the living room that was still surrounded by a ring of pink plastic toys and scraps of wrapping paper. It felt extra fake in the daylight.

Charlie came to pick me up not long after midday. He was wearing new clothes, presents from his mother and father; a soft, grey wool jumper and a new leather jacket, and a waft of unfamiliar aftershave. The smell made me giddy. He kissed me on the cheek when I clambered into the passenger side and handed me a green-and-gold gift bag, tied at the top with a ribbon. I pulled his gift out of my purse, far more interested in his reaction to what I got him than my own reaction to what he got me. I watched him tear the paper off, his face at first confused and then delighted; two tickets to the concert of a band I knew he loved, the kind of band you love in private because the songs mean so much to you that sharing them with your mates would leave you vulnerable. The tickets had been expensive; the most money I'd spent on anyone that Christmas.

—Ya did not.

—I surely did.

—You're a little star. Thanks, babe.

Babe. I turned pink when he kissed me.

—You're welcome. And you can take whoever, it doesn't have to be me.

—Of course it's gonna be you, ya mad egg. Open yours.

I carefully untied the ribbon and set it aside, and found in the bag a Polaroid camera; one of the new model ones in a gorgeous primrose-yellow colour. There were also three packs of film and a box of sweets.

—What are you going spending all that for on me, ya big ejit?

But I was hugging him, tears in my eyes, my seatbelt painfully compressing one of my boobs back into my chest. He laughed, and it rumbled against me, and I murmured a *thank you* into his ear before kissing him. As we pulled off, I started to get nervous at the thought of all the people that'd be in town. Stephen's Night is the busiest night of the year next to New Year's Eve. Chances were I'd run into someone I knew and didn't want to know.

—Who's all gonna be at Connor's?

—Well Connor and Doireann, obviously. Then I think Seány said he'd pop round. Did ya ever meet Connor's brother Jamie? Him and his missus, I can't remember her name.

—It's Aideen.

I had met Jamie and Aideen at the festival. At the time, she had box braids in her very white, very blonde hair, and lip fillers that looked like they might make her mouth explode if she smiled too widely. Jamie was like if the ghost of Tony Montana found himself in the thirty-year-old body of a farmer from Tullamore. They kind of intimidated me; like I was always one dumb comment away from getting kicked up and down the town. I started to quietly regulate my breathing, turned on the radio so Charlie wouldn't hear me, but he noticed. He took his hand off the gear stick and pressed it into mine, unfurling my tightened fist, stretching my palm with his own. *It'll be okay.*

I spent the pre-drinks putting my camera together and testing it out. I had the first pack of film and my wine gone by the time we called a taxi to leave Connor's, gave everyone a memento each, little windows full of happy faces and empty bottles and wisps of smoke. I took an overexposed selfie of Charlie and me and hid it in the back of my purse for safekeeping, our white moon faces squished together, grinning like idiots. I felt the best I'd felt the whole year. I felt unattainably happy. We all climbed into the eight-seater to town. Doireann started a sing-song of 'Fairytale of New York' and we rattled the windows of the taxi and Jim the taxi man let us smoke fags and pass around a naggin of Jameson because he knew Connor's father well. When it got to me, Charlie whispered *please go easy, Sersh* in my ear. I didn't like that but I didn't say anything and passed the naggin to him instead of drinking any. He didn't have any either. He just kissed me on the cheek. My irritation came and went like a solar eclipse.

We were into the pub for four o'clock, the group of us piling in the door, and I felt sickeningly happy to be so a part of something. I wanted to keep up. I wanted to be one of these people, actually be one of the gang, not just Doireann's friend that tagged along, not just hanging around in the perimeters of their lives. I could do it. I could get these people to like me and to want me to be around because I was Saoirse the person, not Saoirse someone who knew someone. I just couldn't do it sober. I queued at the bar alone. I made sure Charlie was outside. I ordered a shot of tequila and sank it. Then I ordered another and sank that too. Then I washed them down with a vodka and lemonade, all of it roiling in my empty stomach, the ring of spilled tequila on the bar top a portent, a warning of a gathering storm.

—Get her up off that table.

—She's grand.

—They're gonna ask us to leave.

—No they're not.

—Man, will ya just get her upright for fuck's sake.

Charlie sighed and gently pulled on my elbow.

—Sersh, you need to sit up or the bouncer is gonna kick us out.

—Fuck him.

—Seriously. Come on. Let's get you a Lucozade or something.

I pulled my chin up off the warm stickiness of the table, an imprint of makeup left behind like the Shroud of Turin.

—Bump sort me right out. Not a bother on me.

—No fuckin' bumps. No more anything. You're cut off.

—You mind your own business, Connor.

The way *Connor* came out of my mouth, you'd swear it was a slur.

—Look at the state of ya, can't even keep your eyes open.

It was true; my eyelids kept drooping closed of their own accord and I had to fight myself to pry them open and keep them that way. I was more than steaming; I was borderline paralytic. I didn't care.

—Where's Doireann?

—She be back in a minute.

—I asked where she was, not when she's back.

—You mind your own business, *Saoirse.*

He spat my name out like a fish bone. I hated him. I hated him more than I'd ever hated anyone. His stupid smug fucking face loomed over the table at me and I could tell he hated me just as much. Panic pricked the back of my neck at not knowing where Doireann was or when she'd gone. I hadn't even noticed. I took out my phone to ring her, struggled with the passcode for a second, eventually just said *phone, ring Doireann.* Connor slapped it out of my hand and it hit the wood with a clatter.

—Hey, hey!

—Control her.

—I'll put your teeth in the back of your throat you ever do that again, man. I mean it.

—Yeah, good one. You won't have any ket then, will ya?

So that's where she was. Gone to Johnjoe to get party favours.

—You let her go to Johnjoe on her own?

—Come on you, we're going for a fag. You fucking pull yourself together before we get back.

It was a struggle to pull myself up from the chair. We went out the back and I put a cigarette in my mouth, tried to light it, realised it was the wrong way round as the acrid smell of burning filter stung my nostrils. Charlie whipped it out of my mouth and stamped on it, put a fresh one between my lips and lit it for me. Jamie and Aideen were shooting me glances; she burst into a peal of laughter when I lit the fag the wrong way round, threw an arm over my shoulder.

—Jasus, what are ya like? Poor little chicken.

Her long, blonde extensions tickled my back and I laughed too, a drunk, stuttery giggle, mouth slackened. I was messy. I was too past the point to do anything about it. We had entered overgrown toddler stages of fucked up. Too fucked up to function. The cigarette made my head spin. I gripped Charlie's arm as he spoke with Jamie, deep in conversation about something I couldn't decipher, except it was about someone named Parsley.

—Why was he called Parsley?

—What?

Charlie looked annoyed.

—Why was his name Parsley? Did his mother call him that or what?

—No. He got sold a bag of parsley once and thought it was weed.

—Oh.

Jamie laughed like it was the funniest thing ever. I didn't find it that amusing. I felt bad for Parsley that a mistake he made probably about a decade ago resulted in a nickname that was going to follow him around for the rest of his life. I was bored now. Aideen's head was in her phone and the lads were chatting and Doireann was still nowhere to be seen. So I quietly slipped off the bar stool and tottered back inside. I ordered another tequila, another vodka. Doireann's friend Kelsey was watching me from the far end of the bar. Her tiny tits were taped into a red dress slashed to her navel and she had an Aperol Spritz in her hand. She said something to one of the girls next to her, and then the both of them were clearly laughing at the spectacle of me. I stuck my middle fingers up at her, smiling, mouthing *fuck you, bitch*, defiant and relishing it, and then she disappeared. My vision and hearing were drowning. I was pressing all my weight into the balls of my feet to prevent tottering. There was simply no way this was going to end well for me. But I could still try to course-correct. I could. I would. I took my shoes off. I went back out to find Charlie. Kelsey had an arm draped around his neck and he was holding her. She was taking a cheeky pull of his fag, sputtering all girly when she handed it back, like *haha, aren't I so naive and beautiful and easy to love.* They were laughing. And then they weren't, because I had a glass full of something in my hand and I was dumping it all over Kelsey. The pub fell silent, Christmas music playing in the eerie suspension of chatter. She started screaming at me, feral, a fistful of my hair in her hand, and then I was screaming too, swinging my shoes like a trunchbull, like it was fucking *EastEnders,* except it wasn't, it was my actual life, and I was actually being dragged shoeless through a pub by Charlie and put outside on the freezing cold footpath. Connor screamed *crazy bitch* as the doors swung shut. I couldn't hear anything then but my own blood pressure rushing in and out of my ears, vomit churning in my stomach. I got sick into a storm drain and people stepped around me.

—Jesus. Saoirse. What did you *do?*

Charlie was angry with me. It made me feel even worse. I got sick again, knees slackening. I sat down on the footpath when it was all out of me. My words were sloppy, slurred.

—I didn't mean to. I'm sorry.

—You're acting like a fucking headcase.

—What does she have that I don't?

—Saoirse, *stop it.* It isn't like that.

—Is it because I'm a headcase and she's normal?

—Don't twist my words.

—Not twisting anything. How long have you been shagging her then?

—I'm not doing this with you right now.

He was ripping my heart into confetti. I couldn't stop the tears when they started. Tequila puke was heavy on my breath. The two metres between us felt like a swollen, broiling river. My pride long gone, I begged him not to leave me.

—You need to go home, Saoirse. I can't talk to you when you're like this.

He flagged down a taxi and I sat on the footpath and bawled. He pulled me up by the forearms and put me into the back, handed the taxi man money and told him my address.

—Please don't leave me alone.

—I'll speak to you when you're sober.

—Charlie.

—The next time you wonder why we're not together, I want you to think of tonight.

He shut the door of the car and stepped back into the pub, never looking back.

———

Everything I've read on childhood trauma suggests that most people subjected to a decade or more of terrible experiences are apt to forget most of it. The details fuzz; the brain takes a big swathe of cloud and obscures the bulk of it, hides the flaws under a sheen of oblivion, makes it hard to pin down if things *really* happened the way they did, if they even happened at all.

This was not my lived experience.

My experience was that I could recall every bad thing that ever happened to little me with scary clarity. I remembered my mother's mascara tears and my father's nicotine fingernails better than I remembered how to count to ten in French or the name of my favourite Jacqueline Wilson book. I took inventory of my trauma as frequently as my brain deemed necessary; usually in bed while trying to fall asleep or during a quiet moment at work or in the car driving somewhere. I would trot out all the old favourites – domestic violence, alcoholism, lack of hot dinners, schoolyard bullies, angry babysitters, dead grandparents, dead pets, dead behind the eyes. I polished these memories like gemstones. I cracked them open like geodes, to examine their hidden shimmering surfaces before glueing them back together. I wanted to forget them and never wanted to let them go at the same time. Who was I, if not the sum of every bad thing that had ever happened to me?

I'd been in bed for three days, moving around at night instead, a friendly ghost that used up teabags and left cereal bowls in the dishwasher and let the dog out for a wee. The house was still awash in Christmas tack, tinsel strung from the light fixtures, cheapening the big oak mantelpiece, wrapped around the banisters of the stairs like a boa constrictor. In the dark I masterfully side-stepped a loose assortment of clunky Barbie Dream Houses, scattered Crayola Twistables and pink Razor scooters abandoned mid-scoot. I picked cold, dry turkey from the carcass sitting in tinfoil in the fridge and ate it with my fingers, leaving them slicked with solidified goose fat. I wrapped myself in the beige shawl-blanket from the sofa and pretended I was the spirit of a jilted Victorian woman, doomed to wander the lofty halls of her ancestral home for all eternity. And when the cloak of the night began to pale almost imperceptibly outside, my pupils shrinking infinitesimally at the light while I sat out on the step and chain-smoked, I knew it was time to go back to bed. All the holes in my heart had now joined together, trunk to tail, a line of elephants meandering through the desert. Since Charlie had stopped speaking to me, he too joined the parade. I dwelt on his rejection to a sickening degree, like a fetishist. I analysed every corner of myself, trying to see me from his eyes. It wasn't hard to guess why he didn't want me anymore. He'd confirmed everything I secretly believed about myself. I wasn't anything special. I worked a minimum wage job and lived at home with no plans extending further than my next payday. I wasn't so pretty that my behaviour could be forgotten about with a quick smile, a flash of tanned cleavage, and a flutter of mink eyelashes. *Why did I have to be the way that I was? Why was I such a stupid drunk bitch with no filter and no manners? Why did I ruin everything?*

When I physically couldn't do it anymore, when it felt like my brain was covered in a layer of wet wool, when I was ready to scratch my skin off, I lay under the sheet, face lit up by the blue light. I typed things like *feeling sick all the time* and *can't get out of bed* and *is pinching a form of self-harm*. I read page after page of WebMD, going from stomach ulcers to ulcerative colitis to Lyme disease to cervical cancer to glioblastoma, stopping only when I got a notification for Instagram. Then I spent what felt like hours clicking aimlessly around the pages of people I knew, then people who knew those people, and then eventually people I didn't know by any degree of separation but whose lives had seemed interesting enough to flick through. Endless, that scrolling, all-consuming, all-swallowing, only stopping when my eyes couldn't keep up or my phone died and I didn't have it in me to reach for the charger on the far side of the bed. This time my phone gave up first; it turned off without me even registering that the battery was low. Then I was alone, in the dark. I didn't need to look out from under the sheet to know it was night-time again. The dark was permeating, spurting like squid ink across the room, diffusing into the air until all was a void again.

New Year's Eve and my twenty-fourth birthday were a couple of days away. I'd always liked being a New Year's baby because it meant every year of my life began and ended with an exact calendar year. I also liked that, no matter who I was with or what I was doing for my birthday, there were champagne and fireworks somewhere. This year, I wanted to forget all about it. I wanted to stay inside my duvet-cave and turn to crumbly old bone while thinking through all the worst things I ever did. Twenty-three had been a fucking disaster so my hopes for twenty-four were exceptionally low. Doireann was still a bit mad at me; Kelsey was her friend, and by all accounts a pretty okay person besides trying to fuck my not-boyfriend. Doireann sent me a pretty bitchy text the day after it happened. *You need to cop on to yourself. She didn't deserve that, Saoirse.* After I read it I had a panic attack. I rolled under the bed and hyperventilated against the debris of my existence, worn socks and loose cigarette filters and empty plastic water bottles all kicked beneath and forgotten about. Usually the week between Christmas and New Year's was my favourite week of the year; nobody knew what day of the week it was, the hours dilated, warped, hazy with food and glitter and snoozing. But the post-binge self-hatred was crippling me. The only reason I might have gotten out of bed during daylight was to wait for death on the floor.

This lasted from the twenty-seventh until the thirtieth. Then there was a knock on the bedroom door.

I deliberately didn't answer. I'd been lying with the covers over my face for a couple of hours, the fabric hot and damp with the condensation from my lungs. The knock came again, and Doireann's voice said *Saoirse*, and I froze myself solid, not breathing, not deigning to make a single sound of life. She would not disturb me. I would let myself fossilise. I was a rock, an endless sheath of permafrost, a column of pure steel—

—I'm coming in.

She tried the handle as she said this but I was clever, I'd locked the door. *Ha, bitch. Gotcha.* There was silence for maybe three minutes before the lock started to click back and forth, and then the handle went again and the door opened this time. I sat up and she stood at the bottom of my bed, triumphant, two bent bobby pins in her upheld hand.

—Thank you, Internet. God, what sort of depression pit is this?

She moved to the window and opened the curtains and I wanted to hiss at her like a feral cat. The light was insulting. How dare the sun keep shining when my life was falling apart?

—I thought ya were dead. Only for I seen your mam in Penneys and she told me you were wallowing.

—Wouldn't you be too? I ruined everything.

—Ah here, pull yourself together would ya.

—Fuck off, Doireann. Just fuck off.

I pulled the covers back over my face. She sat on the bed and yanked them off me.

—If anyone should be telling anyone to fuck off, it's me. Kelsey is raging at me too, you know.

—I don't care.

—Fucking cop on to yourself. Sit up.

I sat up. I looked at her and broke into a watery, wobble-lipped cry. She reached over and wrapped me in a big, warm, sherpa-jacket hug, kissing my hair, running her thumbs underneath my eyes to catch the stray tears.

—You'll be okay. You survived every day of your life so far, you'll survive the next few.

—I'm just so mortified. I never want to leave the house again.

—What, and be stuck here with your mother for all eternity?

—That's a fair point.

—No offence but it smells in here.

She took my dressing gown and towel off the back of the bedroom door and handed them to me.

—Go get a shower. I can't be mates with a cave-dweller, my social standing couldn't take the blow. I'll make the tea.

Showering was an effort, but to my annoyance, it did make me feel better. Not only did the room smell, but I smelled too, like armpit and fake tan and unwashed hair and old drink and cigarettes. I put on music on my phone and had another little cry under the hot water where nobody would be able to tell. When I got out, my room was tidy and the window was open. The bedsheets were stripped and all the half-empty mugs and glasses had been removed. Doireann was an angel on earth. I padded down the stairs in a set of new slipper socks I'd gotten for Christmas, wet hair unbrushed and splayed across the shoulders of my new dressing gown, wan face floating above the thick pink collar like an omen.

—There she is now. Jesus, you look awful.

—Thank you, Mother.

—I just tell it like it is, *a leanbh.*

—Sometimes it'd be nice if you lied.

—You're in the wrong house for a mollycoddling. Act like a vagabond and I'll treat you like one.

She was pissing me off. Doireann gave me a quick look and nodded towards the stairs. I scooped up the mug of tea she'd made me and we started back towards the bedroom. My mother said *okay, see ye later I suppose* in a snarky tone. It took everything in me not to respond impolitely.

Doireann brushed my hair for me patiently, gently, using a boar-bristled brush from her handbag. Then she blow-dried it and straightened it. I hadn't cut it since before I moved back to Ireland; it was long but the ends were deadened, fragile, like straw. I pulled on a jumper and jeans, stuck my feet into my runners. They felt weird in the shoes after days of not even putting on socks. I was back to being something resembling a human. The whole time I was trying to compose myself, Doireann was chattering.

—Me and Connor had a woeful kick-off after you left. Even Charlie had a go at him.

Charlie's name was a needle prick.

—What happened?

—Well Connor was slagging you, and Charlie told him to shut up, and then Connor kinda like pushed him? Like elbowed him to get to me, and sure you know me, I started roaring at him about being ignorant. Then he called me a stupid bitch and I called him a stupid bastard and we called the whole thing off again even though we were never officially a thing. I didn't even have a cry this time. Just downloaded Tinder again in the taxi home. Fuck him.

—Charlie stuck up for me?

—Yeah… He's big mad at you though, girlypop, I won't lie to you. I dunno how you're gonna fix that.

I felt sick. I pivoted.

—What does that even mean by the way? Never *officially* together?

—We're like together but not *together*-together.

—So you do all the things a couple does without the security of knowing you're not gonna get cheated on.

—That's a very uptight view. It's just whatever. I don't tie him down, he doesn't tie me down, it's grand like.

—And you don't want anything more than that?

—Not really. Sometimes I think it'd be nice, but then I like being my own woman too.

—Have you been seeing other lads?

—Well no. Well I kissed that fella at the festival. But we were broken off then.

I didn't ask if Connor had been seeing other women, because I already knew he was. This entire line of thought was vexing and embarrassing to me. I hadn't wanted to so much as touch off anyone but Charlie since the minute he kissed me for the first time. If I found out he was seeing other girls regularly I'd probably have killed myself. I thought back to the festival again, about the smell of perfume on his jacket, about Kelsey, about her touching him, about me running at her. I felt vile. I'd tried to call him the day after Stephen's Day but it didn't even ring out. His phone was off. So I sent him an apologetic message and asked him to ring me. He'd never even opened it. He'd been on his phone since because I'd check periodically; *Active 47 mins ago. Active 3 mins ago. Active now.* My message remained unread.

Doireann and I took Max for a walk around the lake. The weather was dry but a misery all the same; threatening to precipitate at any given moment, cold but humid so you were sweating in your parka after five minutes of movement. Max was old and moved slow, thankfully. The daylight made my eyes smart.

—What are we doing for your birthday then?

—*I'm* doing fuck all.

—Don't be like that.

—I mean it. I'm swore off drink after Stephen's Day.

—It should actually be illegal to have your birthday on New Year's and not go out.

—If it was, I'd break the law. I don't give a shit.

—Ah go on! Don't be dry. Sure I'll mind ya.

After another fifteen minutes of berating, I agreed to go out. Maybe it was better if I didn't sit in and wallow. It hadn't done me any favours so far.

———

—Do you think they'll be out tonight?

—Probably.

I was panicky, and no amount of wine could quell it. The last thing I wanted to verbally fixate on was Charlie and Connor, but Doireann couldn't let it go.

—If he's out, I'm ignoring him. He can fuck off.

—Mhmm.

She turned from her makeup mirror to eye me.

—What's wrong with you?

—Nothing, just tired.

—Well that's a lie. Is it Charlie? Did ya hear anything from him?

—I don't want to talk about it.

—So that's a no then.

—I literally just said I didn't want to talk about it. I'll be sick if I have to talk about it anymore, Doireann.

I physically couldn't think of anything but Charlie but even saying his name was like chewing glass.

—That's no attitude to start your new year with.

She might have talked a big game, but Doireann was a pillar of unshakeable faith in other human beings. I just kept drinking and breathing mindfully; according to Dr Google, in for four, hold for seven, out for eight was a useful tool for calming down. It just made me dizzy.

Doireann and I arrived at the doors of the pub at ten. I was already buzzed; three glasses of wine as I got ready in her house had me floating, bouncing up the footpath. She took the fifty note from my hand at the bar and I ordered us drinks while she weaved her way through to the smoking area, on the hunt for Johnjoe who'd surely be propping up the back bar. As I waited for our two vodka whites I pulled out my phone, checked to see if Charlie was online. He was. He still hadn't opened my message. The sight of the little green dot was offensive. *Active.* Actively ignoring me. Maybe he was out tonight. Maybe he was out with another girl. Maybe I'd run into them somewhere and maybe I'd have a worse broken heart to nurse alongside my hangover tomorrow. Maybe I wouldn't let it get that far.

The crowd was making me nervous; I pinched the insides of my bare biceps hard, rolling the soft flesh between my fingernails until it ached and itched. When the barman came back with the glasses and the half-filled bottle of flat white lemonade I necked the vodka straight from one and ordered another, handing him my bank card. The ice hit my teeth with a chink and I suppressed a shudder, swallowing hard, eyes watering, lipstick on the back of my hand when I wiped my mouth. I hadn't learned anything. Already I was close to slurring but the faces were coagulating now, blurring, further away. I found Doireann with her head thrown back laughing, her skin glistening under the red light of the patio lamps. She was probably the prettiest girl I'd ever been friends with. It did not do wonders for my self-esteem. Another gulp of syrupy vodka-lemonade and I tugged on the strap of her handbag.

—It's in the little zip pocket on the inside.

—Do you want to come with me?

—No, I'm in the middle of something here.

The man in front of her was watching her, rapt, a finger on the rim of his pint and his feet pointed in her direction. He was wearing eyeliner and I had to swallow a laugh when

I looked at him. She took her drink from me and kissed me on the cheek, leaving a sticky lip gloss ring beneath my eye. I stuck my hand inside her purse and grasped the baggie with the tips of my fingers, curling my fist tight like a stone all the way to the bathroom.

An hour and a half later and I was sparkling. *For a good time, call me.* The coke balanced out the drink nicely, kept me upright, maybe a little too loud at times but charming all the same. The man who'd taken a shine to Doireann followed us to the nightclub with his three friends in tow. They were in a band together. They wore rings and low v-necks and sunglasses indoors and had opinions on which Gallagher brother was the best one. I hated them all, particularly the bassist who kept trying to buy me a birthday drink. When I was ordering, he put a hand on the small of my back and tried to say something sexy in my ear but the music was, thankfully, too loud to make it out. I side-stepped him, drank both of the shots I ordered and went to dance.

Then, nothing.

And then, the bathroom. My underwear around my ankles and the dial tone in my ear and someone banging on the cubicle door. My birthday sash was crumpled and hanging around my neck like a yoke. Sick on my thighs, sick on the floor. I wiped it off my legs with one rubber hand, wadded with tissue. Tried to stand up, fell back onto the seat with a slap, heard the hinges crack and break. I stood again, gripping the toilet paper dispenser for stability, and opened the door. A girl I didn't know stood there with her arms crossed.

—I missed the countdown because of you.

I stumbled out, checked myself in the mirror, forehead pressed against the cool glass; the left side of my neck had a bite mark that was rapidly purpling, and it ached, and I couldn't remember how it got there. A dull, far-away panic sounded in me. By some divine miracle I made my way to the exit, through the throng of people with balloons and streamers and cocktails, all kissing and dancing and laughing, and fumbled in my bra for my cloakroom ticket, trying so desperately to focus, to stay aware long enough to get into a taxi and back to Doireann's. And then, again, the hand on the small of my back and the voice in my ear. But I could hear him this time.

—Come on, let's get you home.

The walls spun and I fought to keep my eyes open. Jacket in hand, I teetered on the top of the steps, a pyramid with me Blu-tacked to the tip. The double doors below us were open onto the street, and I heard what I thought was Charlie, walking by with his friends, laughing, and I had to get to him, I had to get him to talk to me, to hear me say how sorry I was, to tell him I loved him more than I loved myself or anyone else, that I was miserable every second I had to live in the knowledge that he didn't want me anymore. I just wanted him to love me.

The bassist, working harder now to get me to move, lifted his arm so he was supporting my weight. Those dull, familiar alarm bells rang again – feminine instinct telling me to run the fuck in the opposite direction of the man in front of me because every facet of his behaviour felt like it was veiling a threat, a bruise, a bite mark.

I summoned all my remaining strength and pushed against him, weakly, but it was unexpected enough that he let go suddenly. I stumbled again in the shoes, my ankle rolling, sending me face first into the handrail. I felt my front tooth snap clean in two on impact, heard a scream that wasn't mine.

And then, nothing again.

V

I woke up with violence.

I'd been dreaming of a house that was all my childhood houses stitched together, running down halls that dead-ended, staring out windows that hung over chasms. On a false step, I slipped off the edge of a staircase and fell into consciousness, gasping, eyes fighting for focus. My throat felt like I'd swallowed a handful of cat claws; when I lifted my hand to touch my mouth, the crook of my elbow prickled and stuck, a drip dug into the vein at an angle. That was worrying. I looked up. I was in a hospital ward, and someone had their hand on my shoulder, trying to push me onto the pillow.

—You're alright, pet. Lie back there and I'll call the nurse.

My father's wrinkling, earnest face turned from me towards the call bell, and in a fit of sudden fatigue I sank back, trying to gather my bearings. I tried to recall the last thing I could properly remember, pulling thoughts out of the fog. Getting to the pub. And then... *what the fuck had happened then?* I went to lick my lips and, to my horror, found I was missing half my left front tooth and a lump from my right. My top lip was stitched up to the Cupid's bow; it seared and ached when I moved my mouth and I wondered how I hadn't immediately noticed. Did I get hit by a car? Beaten with a hurl? Fall off a bridge?

—What happened to me?

The words came out gargled, strangled.

—What?

—What happened to me?

—Christ, daughter. You do take after me.

The nurse came barrelling through the ugly green-and-orange curtains, all bustle, little cart of horrors in tow, and my father sat back into the visitor's chair to give her space.

—Well you finally decided to grace us with your sentience, did you, missy? How are we feeling?

—Why am I here?

—Why are you here? You had a little tumble, but I'm not surprised you don't recall. We pumped enough out of you to get the whole town drunk. Now leave those alone or they'll heal wonky – hand down.

She gently but firmly pulled my hand away from my face, where I had been probing the stitches with clumsy, trembling fingers. When I spoke, my tongue scraped against the jagged corners of my broken incisors. Panic stabbed me in the chest. *Oh Christ, what did I do?* The nurse, whose lanyard said Pauline, was wrapping a blood pressure cuff around my right bicep while eyeing the IV bag above me.

—That's your second bag of saline. Feeling fresh yet?

—Just peachy, thanks.

—Any aches or pains?

I nodded and gestured limply towards my face.

—I'll grab you some painkillers when I finish up.

As the cuff inflated, pushing my pulse to the surface of my wrist, she clipped a monitor to my finger and stuck a thermometer in my ear before taking notes on a clipboard.

—Well you'll survive anyway. The doctor does her rounds before lunch, I'd say she'll send you packing, so, Dad, if you want to sort her some clothes?

My father nodded and she disappeared again. I was still desperately trying to remember and coming up with nothing but flecks of dust. It didn't take a genius to understand I'd overdone it in a big way. My father was idly tapping at his phone, posture relaxed.

—Your mother is going to drop in a bag for you in an hour or two.

—You were talking to her?

He held up the phone to show me their texts, curt little messages containing the barest, most necessary of information regarding my consciousness or lack thereof. Her number wasn't saved.

—Is she raging with me?

—She'll get over it. Do you remember what happened at all?

—No.

I was mortified to admit it. Tears gathered in my lashes.

—You had a fall down the stairs in the bar. A bouncer called the ambulance and the hospital called me. They had to pump your stomach, so in a way it's lucky you took the tumble or you might have died in your sleep anyway.

I looked at him. His face had aged in the time we'd been estranged. Sun damage dug deep lines into his forehead and around his eye sockets. His broad back had a stiffness to it when he moved, sore from stooping to turn mulch, to lay sod. He looked hungover. His good shirt and jeans were wrinkled from the night in the hospital chair. He'd definitely come straight here from the pub. For once, I wished my mother was there. The nurse returned with two fizzy codeine and a cup of water. I fought the urge to gag, drank it, and closed my eyes again.

My father placed his hand gently on my forearm as I fell back into the abyss.

———

When I was five years old, I got the chickenpox from Doireann. My very first memory of being ill is when I had the chickenpox. I was rashy, miserable. My father never had them as a child so he'd sequestered himself in Granny Maher's house for a week while Máire and I stayed in our flat. I spent a lot of time whimpering and feeling sorry for myself, things that usually irritated my mother. She was a different person when I was sick, slipping into the skin of a caring matriarch. She stuck oven mitts to my tiny, itchy hands to stop me from flaying myself as I slept. She let me lay my head in her lap while she pressed a cold cloth to my neck, my scalp, the backs of my knees. She kept calamine lotion in the freezer and rubbed it into my skin, circular and shocking. She let me stay up late to watch *What Ever Happened to Baby Jane?* She whisper-sang to me until I fell asleep. My entire life, whenever I was sick, I couldn't help but want my mother. I wanted her when I woke up in the hospital that day, teeth in bits, face purple and black and yellow and angry red. I wanted her when they took out the cannula and my blood shot out of the vein and hit the nurse in the apron. I wanted her especially when my father took his leave.

She didn't come in with the bag; my father met her out front to collect it for me. When the doctor gave me the all-clear to go home after my drip was emptied, he gave me twenty euros for a taxi, side-hugged me and kissed me on the top of my head, and went. Someone had put all my things into a big clear plastic bag and left them at the foot of the bed; my clothes, shoes, and purse all stank of puke, and the front of my dress was crusty with dried blood. I dug my phone out and felt relief to see it was dead. My knees and left hip were papered with bruises, aching under the fabric of the leggings Máire dropped in. The hoodie she left was Charlie's; it smelled of him so innately that I buried my face into the fabric like a little kid. I'd have to come back to get the stitches out, and to maybe talk about a plastic surgeon, depending on how I healed. Calling the dentist would have to wait until they opened again. My teeth were atrocious. I examined them in the tiny mirror of the ward bathroom, hidden under the pulpy mess of my top lip, the edges jagged, the gums nearly black with trauma. There was a bite mark on the side of my neck, different to the other contusions, two neat arcs of teeth dug into the skin. I remembered a flash, a foggy sliver of the night before, my eyes rolling around in my head, my neck aching dully. I knew it wasn't Charlie and that's all I knew. The bathroom spun. My hands shook violently as I dropped one between my legs to check, to feel, to make sure. Nothing there to suggest. Nothing to say something worse. I closed my eyes and sat on the floor until the nurse came by and knocked.

My stomach had been aching from the minute I opened my eyes and got worse and worse the closer I got to Máire's house. When I disembarked at her doorstep, the taxi man wished me a Happy New Year. I almost laughed into his face. I took the key from under the pot of the giant aloe at the front door and let myself in quietly, the click of the closing door echoing out into the empty hall. Nobody was home. I filled a hot-water bottle, made tea, took two more painkillers. I had to drink my tea lukewarm and through a plastic straw. I tried a mouthful of cold water and screeched like a dying owl. I plugged my phone in but left it off. *Why couldn't I remember anything?* Eventually I could track myself as far as paying into the nightclub. After that, a flash of the dancefloor. A toilet cubicle with a broken seat. Someone's hand on my back. The taste of blood. Everything else was a void, and I poured my mental energy into it, trying to grab even a tendril of context. I'd have to ring Doireann. I couldn't face it. I didn't really need the details, anyway. The end result was the same. The Solpadol kicked in quickly on my empty stomach. I fell asleep sitting up in the bed.

When I woke up, it was dark. I was in a disgusting amount of pain. I needed more codeine. I took my empty glass, speckled inside with Solpadol remnants like a broken snowglobe, and limped to the bathroom. The girls' bedroom doors were closed. So was Máire and JJ's. There wasn't a sound. I filled my glass from the bathroom tap with the light still off so I wouldn't see my face in the mirror. When I got back to the room, I realised I'd left the painkillers down in the kitchen. I debated trying to sleep through the incessant stab ripping up through my mouth. I decided I couldn't and hobbled down the stairs as quietly as I could. I saw my mother sitting at the kitchen counter, an iota too late to turn back. She had a glass of wine and a magazine in front of her. She gasped at the sight of me.

—Oh Jesus, Saoirse. *Jesus.*

—It's not that bad.

—Your face. What did you do to your beautiful *face?*

She reached out and then recoiled. She couldn't look away from me. I didn't want her to see me anymore. I turned towards where I'd left the tablets and grabbed them, my hands shaking again.

—Look at me.

—Why? So you can make me feel even worse?

My words were coming out all funny. My lips and teeth couldn't shape the sounds right, air whistling through the hole where the ends of my incisors should be. She was beside me then. She turned me by the shoulders to face her. She cupped my jaw in her cold hand. Her eyes and mine, shining, searching for something. She dropped her hand and started to cry.

—When are you going to fucking grow up, Saoirse?

I didn't have an answer.

———

Granny Lynch died on a cold morning at the end of January.

The care worker who found her was new enough on the job. Granny was her first dead one, and when we pulled up to the nursing home she was still outside, chain-smoking and shaking, her face pink and raw from crying. My mother had also been crying; her knees gave out in the kitchen and I'd had to help her off the floor, had to call around the aunties as we sped over to the Willows Retirement Community, Máire silent and white while I searched numbers and repeated the words *it's Máire's daughter Saoirse, the nursing home called, Granny passed away.* I stayed in the car with the girls while Máire went in, awkwardly waving to each of my aunties as they pulled up either side, Imelda's hair only half-brushed, Philomena's mouth set in a grim slant.

The removal was long, drawn-out, our maudlin faces gathered around Granny Lynch's corpse, shaking hands with what felt like the whole town. I didn't feel right, sitting there, grasping hand after caring hand; the empathy was not mine to receive, but my mother insisted I sit next to her. If Philomena's and Imelda's eldest children would be sitting there and sympathising then by God so would hers. A cousin offered me a brandy, and I hesitated before ultimately turning it down, running my tongue over my new teeth almost compulsively. JJ and Máire had had to foot my dental bill. I didn't have four grand sitting around for new front teeth. The guilt of it made my mouth ache. I stuck to tea, hot, dark, made from Granny's stovetop tea kettle with a half-century's worth of limescale and tannin built up on the inside. After an hour of gawping faces and murmured *very sorry*'s, Doireann arrived. She did the rounds solemnly, shaking my cousin Tadhg's hand a little too long. She blessed herself going by Granny. Then she shot me a look and I excused myself, avoiding the disapproving gaze of my mother, and snuck out for a cigarette with her. It was my first time seeing her since my fall. She'd already called me and filled me in on what she knew of New Year's, which really began and ended with *you were there and then you were gone.* She asked for a good look at my new teeth and told me they were nicer than my original ones. It was dark out; I could see in the front window without being seen. Granny Lynch's nose was the only part of her visible to me, a small, waxy yellow mushroom growing from the bright, polished oak of the coffin.

—Jesus, you've had a month of it.

—Don't even start.

—Your cousin's a ride. He single?

—That is… incredibly inappropriate.

—Hey, grief brings people together.

Not always. I'd hoped Charlie would message me when he saw the RIP.ie link I reposted to Instagram, but he was still in the wind. The self-absorption of worrying about my love life at my grandmother's funeral wasn't lost on me but I couldn't really think about anything else. And I fucking tried.

Before the hearse arrived to take her to the church, we were all encouraged to sit with Granny Lynch alone, to say our goodbyes. I had nothing to say, except that I was sorry I never visited again. They'd taken one of her headscarves and tucked it around her neck, wrapped her dusky pink rosary beads between her fingers, hands one on top of the other, stiff and unfeeling. Someone had pinned her Pioneers badge to her bolero cardigan, a flaming sacred heart on a white shield. I remembered then the sharp tang of rye off her breath as she leaned over me one tense Christmas, right before Imelda carted her off to bed. At her funeral, a grandchild from each sister gave a reading. My voice shook as I stood at the podium, eyes glued to the sheet, wishing for all the world I could have had a drink beforehand. I tried to speak the words at a normal speed. *A time to live and a time to die. A time to sow and a time to reap.* The readings had no bearing on any aspect of my grandmother's life, besides the fact that she was a staunch Catholic. It felt impersonal and rote; stand up, bless yourself, sit down, priest reads, stand up again, sit down again, parishioner reads, Communion, shake hands, leave. JJ, three of my cousins, and my aunts' husbands carried Granny to the graveyard. It wasn't women's work to carry a coffin, apparently. Máire was crying silently the entire slow, agonising walk. Imelda was crying loudly. Philomena, the eldest, simply kept everything on track, no time to cry.

Following the woman who created us all to her grave, surrounded by people who had the same nose or eyes or freckles as me, I felt as outside of everything as I'd ever been. My counsellor called it *derealisation*.

———

Due to the infamy of my drunken fall – stable people don't black out and break teeth, according to Doireann – I'd started seeing a counsellor. It was probably for the best; I hadn't been doing well at all since it had happened. I'd spent my nights hugging my knees and watching episode after episode of *Teen Mom*, eyes on the laptop until the sun rose, drifting off and jolting awake every now and again, sometimes crying.

Being awake during the day had been becoming less and less essential, and I hadn't left the house unless Doireann brought me into town for 'groceries' – really she was doing recon to make sure I wasn't going to kill myself. I wasn't, but only because I didn't think I had the energy to do a proper job of it. It was like when I dropped out of college all over again. I stopped going to work and when Rosie or Nadia called me, I didn't answer. My GP had prescribed me antidepressants after an appointment I'd made because I stayed up all night convincing myself I had a brain tumour. The pale green script for Lexapro sat unfilled in the bottom of my handbag, accumulating crumbs of dirt and indelible creases. I was resistant to accepting that there was anything wrong with me until one early morning I heard all three of my sisters knock gently and out of time on my bedroom door. A part of me itched to open it, but depression sunk me into the mattress. I lay still and quiet until I was sure they were gone to school and got up to use the toilet, but when I opened the door, on the floor was a cold, milky cup of tea in the mug they gave me for Christmas, blackened toast with jam spread haphazardly, and a small pile of drawings – a butterfly with big, purple wings, a chicken-scratch rendition of Max the dog, and a portrait of who I thought was supposed to be me, my crooked legs unequal lengths, a void black curve for a smile, a pair of yellow-circle hoop earrings on the sides of my moon-round face. That was the morning I found a therapist.

Lisa-Anne had a five-star rating on Google. That was good enough for me. Over email, I made an appointment for the following Monday and proceeded to consider cancelling it every hour of every day up until I was standing in her waiting room. She had jasmine incense lit and Lyric FM playing from a plug-in radio, and little affirmations hung around the walls, dotted between her accreditations; *every day may not be good but there is good in every day*, a cursive iteration of *everyone's journey is different*, and of course, the old reliable *in for 4, hold for 7, out for 8*. I considered leaving but I'd had to ring a camera bell to get in so she'd already seen me, and an unwillingness to let down Lisa-Anne, a woman who I'd never met and who I owed nothing, kept me in the waiting room until I was called.

Tall and thin, Lisa-Anne looked exactly like the type of woman to light incense in a place of business. Her hair, black with an occasional grey, fell in a long, soft plait down the back of her dress, a floaty, high-necked, long-sleeved, maxi-skirt affair in a pattern that can only be described as seventies-curtain, but it suited her. She made it work. She had the aura of my mother's cool childless aunt who only visited on holidays bearing souvenirs from far-flung corners of the world. We sat across from each other in mismatched, overstuffed chairs, between us a low coffee table bearing nothing but Kleenex and Lisa-Anne's reusable coffee cup. She asked me to tell her about myself and I had nothing to say but *I live at home and I used to live in London*.

—Why did you come to me today?

—My friend thinks I'm depressed.

—Why does your friend think that?

—I don't know… I guess I haven't been sleeping well.

When Lisa-Anne had said nothing, I'd felt compelled to fill the void. And suddenly, words had started pouring out of my mouth at an alarming rate, about Charlie and losing my job, and my father and my sisters and my mother, oh, my mother, sentences and paragraphs and soliloquies devoted to Máire, and before I'd known it I was snotty from crying and Lisa-Anne had been gently trying to bring the session to an end. That night, I'd left a Kinder Bueno on each of my sisters' pillows and slept, unbroken, for a whole three hours.

My mother hadn't really spoken to me until Granny Lynch died, and even then it was curt, clipped sentences to pass on vital information and to pass herself in front of her family. But still, she'd brought me to get my stitches out at the hospital. She'd driven me to my teeth appointments and stayed with me as the dentist probed and pulled and filed and glued. She'd given over the credit card at the front desk but said nothing when I said thank you, my face hot and half-numb. She loved me because I was her child. She was furious with me for the same reason. As the days wore on and the tension grew, her silence weighed on me like wet wool. I'd tried, more than once, to engage her – my thoughts on *Little Women*, offers of coffee, comments on the weather – and every time it was like I'd spoken only to hear my own voice hit the walls. When the funeral was over, we all went back to Imelda's for sandwiches and soup. And apparently, wine. My mother started drinking and the drinking made her feel even more sorry for herself and with more drink that self-pity turned into some sort of seething rage that she began to bleed into every room she entered. She kept contradicting people as they shared a memory or a story about Granny; *no, no, sorry now, Jim, I'll have to stop you there, because my mother would never have eaten a kiwi with the skin on. No, that's not how she used to fold down the bedsheets. Sure how would you remember if she hit me with the wooden hanger or not when you weren't even there?* Philomena actually asked me to bring her home. I couldn't believe it. I had to call JJ to come back and pick us up. I tried not to sound smug. We'd been banished to wait out by the gate for him, Máire swaying in the wind like a dandelion. When we got into the house, the dam broke. She was wounded. She started on me. *Are you gonna keep wasting your life? Are you not ashamed of yourself? Do you know how much money we had to pay the dentist for you? Do you know I had people in work asking me about your 'accident'? I had to lie, Saoirse. The shame of it.* On and on and on she went, and I kept ignoring her, mute, pretending she wasn't following me into every room I entered as I got ready to go to bed. When she tried to follow me into the bathroom I sped up and swung the door closed. She shoved her foot in the jamb and wedged it back open.

—Get out of my way, Saoirse.

—No.

Gee-eyed, she stood in the doorway with her face bulging against the jamb, so close to me that her spittle hit my cheek as she spoke through her teeth.

—I threw away my life, gave up every part of me, to keep you. Do you realise? Do you even care what I had to miss out on? I never got to go to college, or see the world, or get so drunk I smashed my own bloody face in. Because I had *you* to think about. Nobody was gonna come pick me up off the ground, pay my hospital bills, give me a place to live. My mother wouldn't even speak to me until you were nearly two.

—I didn't fucking ask to be here.

I knew it was petty, something a stroppy teenager would say mid-tantrum. But it was true. Nobody ever knocked on the wall of the womb as I lay in there and asked me if I wanted to be born into this chaos. If they had, I'd have said a resounding *no*. I stepped back from the door abruptly and she stumbled in the absence of my resistance, still spitting her words at me.

—There you go again. So ungrateful. Your own mother's suffering means that little to you, when all I've done for the past twenty-four years is worry about you.

—Please. It's not like you've given a single shit about me since Lily came along. You forgot you had four fucking kids right to my face.

That did it. She swung her arm and slapped me clean across the jaw, hard enough to make my hearing ring a little. It stunned me for a split second, and then I felt my own hand twitch, my shoulder taut with unused tension, and I had to dig my nails into my palm to stop myself from hitting her back. Her eyes, like her own mother's, like mine, were savage, blue and defiant, nude lipstick smeared at the corner of her lips, her teeth set wildly, bottom ones overlapping top, and her chest heaving with big, hard breaths. The smell of wine hung between her mouth and mine.

—I won't forget that.

—Good.

Pink spit hissed through her gritted incisors.

—Feel proud of yourself, Mother? Feel like the big woman now?

Her eyes widened and she lifted her arm again, but this time I caught her by the wrist as her open hand sailed towards me, cleaving the air like the prow of a ship. She raised the other hand and I grabbed that too, and there we stood, her half a foot shorter than me, both of us arms up, joined like we were playing a game of London Bridge. I could feel the fury thrumming in her pulse, the rage, the disappointment that, in the end, I had turned out just like the both of them.

—Get out of my house. You can be your father's problem for a change.

—No bother. Wouldn't want to stay anywhere I'm not welcome, Máire.

I let go of her arms and flew out of the bathroom, up the stairs, slapping the big heavy shell of my suitcase onto her stupid floor, and started pelting things into it: clothes, shoes, laptop, hair dryer, makeup, whatever came under my hand next. When it was full, I stomped on it to get the zip shut before grabbing my backpack and filling that with my essentials: passport, birth cert, phone charger, cigarettes. The drawings my sisters left outside my door were now tacked to the wall next to the bed. I slowed my ire to take them down carefully, folded them with the reverence of a wedding dress, and tucked them into the sleeve of a book. Then I unplugged my lamp and pulled it from the bedside table. I didn't even look back at the room. I didn't have everything, but anything left behind meant nothing to me anyway. I slid the suitcase down the stairs on its side, hoping it'd take hunks out of the wooden steps, scratch the banisters so deep they'd have to replace them, leave cracks and holes in the drywall. They'd have to do the work to rid this house of me.

—She's damaging our property, JJ, she's kicking lumps out of the stairs and the walls and everything, I don't know what to do.

My mother held her mobile phone to her ear, her breath a hiccup now, her voice a falsetto. I brushed past her into the kitchen to grab my mug from the press, the one the girls had given me, wrapping it in paper towels before I put it in my bag. I didn't hear her until she was right beside me, trying to pry the mug from me, the kitchen tissue crumpling and ripping.

—That's not yours.

—My sisters gave it to me so yeah, it is mine.

—I fucking paid for it so you can let go of it.

Instead, I gripped tighter, resisted the urge to sweep her legs out from under her with my foot, and soon we were trying to wrench it from each other's hands, and she was pushing me into the cabinets with the side of her body, surprisingly difficult to get out from under, and then the mug slipped from between us and hit the tile floor with a deafening, inorganic crack. We both froze and looked down; the delicately painted pieces were asunder on the floor, the gentle purple swirls and petals all split apart like a daisy crushed under a cow hoof.

—Now look, *look* at what you've done.

She sprung to action, on her hands and knees picking up the splinters, hissing when her finger began to drip blood. I did look, for a moment. Then I left.

On my way out to the road, I could see Lily's bedroom light was on, and there, in the window, were the silhouettes of my sisters in descending height, fuzzy halos of hair and little hands pressed against the glass. I loosened my death-grip on the suitcase for a moment and waved, one-handed and weak, before starting off into the night.

I walked for a while, aimlessly. I could have called someone, Doireann or my father or even Charlie if I was desperate enough, but I didn't want to. I'd been enough of a burden. I was tired of weighing other people down. So I walked, and dragged my suitcase, and smoked fags, and walked, and walked and walked, the weight of my lamp in my hand, the roads well lit by the luminance of a newly waning moon. Eventually I ended up outside my father's mother's house, a subconscious migration back to the place I felt safest, like a swallow roosting in the sun-warmed eaves of a turf shed. It was still dark. It was still empty. The key was still under Mary's serpent-bound feet. All of the weeds were dead with the winter frosts. I turned on the flashlight on my phone and let myself in for the last time. I stood still for a moment to ensure no rats were skittering. There was only silence, eerie and all-consuming. I picked a path through to my grandmother's bedroom, pausing here and there to take in the remains of my childhood, shoes reverberating on the dirty terrazzo flooring, once coated in a thin, threadbare layer of carpet. I was a patron in the gallery of my own life. In the kitchen was the table I ate a thousand dinners at. By the range was the armchair I napped in. By the back door was where Pip the dog died and taught me of the impermanence of life. Over on the collapsed sofa was where my father lay smelling of stout and drooling. In the spare bedroom was where my mother and I stayed when we had nowhere else to go.

Granny Maher's room was stripped of anything worth having. The bedframe was rusted and creaking, the mattress long gone. I sat in against the wall and watched the moon continue its arc across a sky that wouldn't begin to pale for another few hours. I tried not to think of spiders and wood-worm and rat piss. I tucked the bottom half of my face inside my scarf to block out the smell of mould and rotting wall-paper. I didn't fall asleep. Instead I just sat there and waited for something I couldn't identify to take root inside of me and propel me to leave again. Maybe it would never come. Maybe they'd find me here in a few weeks, sucked into the walls, encased in the stone like a raw amethyst, glittering and broken and cursed.

———

Living in Doireann's house was like visiting Mars.

Every morning, without fail, her mother knocked gently on her door to wake us up. Not once in the months I lived there did I ever see her set an alarm. On Fridays, her father drove her car to the Applegreen and filled it with petrol, checked her tyre pressure and drove it back to the house for her. Nobody ever shouted, the mood was never sour, her parents never fought. Well, not in front of me anyway. They *were* sleeping in separate rooms, but I didn't think it was polite to ask Doireann why. I had to share her room with her as a result. She was a sprawler, but I didn't have to pay rent so it was a fair trade.

In the worst weeks of my spiral, I hadn't showed up to work for like a fortnight. Understandably, I'd been fired. I wasn't even mad about it. I would have fired me too. Granny Lynch's will had a thousand euros in it for each of her nine grandchildren. Mine went straight to my escape fund, which was reaching a tidy little sum until I was let go. But then Doireann got me a job with her. I made coffee and served muffins and wiped down tables three days a week. Most of my money went into my savings but I gave her mother and father sixty euros every Friday for my share of the groceries and bills. Karen would get me to make a little list of things I specifically wanted and she'd add them into her weekly shop. When I was working a shift without Doireann, Karen would drop me into town on her way to work in the hospital. She was very gentle with me. Probably because Doireann had told her what happened with Máire. Or maybe because my face still looked a little fucked up and she pitied me. I could cover the angry pinkness of the scar fairly well with makeup, but without it my mouth was a state. The surgeon said I wouldn't need any work done to it. It was fairly super-ficial, in the end. I just had to be patient. Patience wasn't one of my virtues.

I hadn't gone on a night out since my accident. I was afraid to drink and mortified at the thought of showing my face in the town in that way again. Any time I felt like I was missing out I just ran my tongue over the lump of scar tissue on the inside of my top lip, like Braille spelling out *not worth it.* I still got great big pangs of shame when I thought about it, but I knew eventually it would go away if I stopped dwelling on it. Counselling was a hoot; the more I went the worse I felt, and then suddenly the better I felt, like flossing with gingivi-tis; initially it fucking hurt but with regular upkeep, I'd stop spitting blood. When I had an appointment I spent the whole day beforehand feeling like I might have a panic attack, and after the appointment, wherein I'd bitch and moan and complain about my terrible parents and terrible childhood and terrible adulthood, I'd feel like sleeping for a week, purged of all the anxious bile that ran my body ragged.

During my third visit to her office, Lisa-Anne recommended I take up a hobby. *What do you like to do?* I didn't really have an answer for her. I'd been taking my antidepressants for a week, on her recommendation, and I felt like shit. My brain was slow to grease its wheels and now it was all I could do not to fall asleep. I thought for a minute, letting the now-comfortable silence sit between us. I liked to go drinking; it embarrassed me that this was the first thing to enter my head. I strained, picking apart past afternoons in search of something I enjoyed doing. I liked walking, and drinking hot beverages, and watching movies alone in the dark, but none of those seemed like the right answer, the answer she was looking for. For 'homework', she recommended I think back to childhood and remember all the things I filled my spare time with, to see if anything caught a spark. I was dubious.

When I arrived at my father's doorstep this is what I was thinking about. I was methodically running through pastimes in my head and crossing them off out of disinterest or incapability. Watersports? *Pointless in middle Ireland.* Knitting? *I'd rather be dead.* Drawing? *Requires a natural level of talent that I most certainly do not possess.* Baking? *Christ, will I start sporting a pinny and rollers too?* The childhood recommendation was a dead end; adults don't play with dolls. Not the outwardly normal ones anyway. I used to read a lot. Maybe I'd pick up a book or two. Maybe I'd just think about it and not bother doing it, like most things.

A humid breeze was about; to walk into it hurt my mouth, made the nerves bristle and prick. I could feel my pulse in my front teeth. I put a hand to my mouth instinctively, the flesh still psychosomatically tender. I realised that I had been standing in front of the house for almost five minutes and hadn't knocked. The door was adorned with a wrought-iron knocker in the shape of a fleur-de-lis and the wood had recently been painted a deep forest green; speckles of the paint had sprayed onto the concrete step and looked like the tips of grass blades beneath me, boring up through the grey. The windows all had terracotta-shaded plastic window boxes, filled with pansies in vibrant ochre, violet, and crimson. The clusters of flowers offended me. My hand twitched as I thought of grabbing two fistfuls of them and ripping them out before throwing them into the ditch. I hoped to Christ she wasn't in there. His landscaping van was parked out the front. Through the passenger window I could see an old disposable coffee cup, stained brown on the rim; a crushed Benson & Hedges box in the seat, on top of a copy of some newspaper opened to the racing pages. There was dried cement smeared into the dull grey of the seat fabric. Fifteen minutes now, approaching twenty. I lit a cigarette and looked at the knocker as I smoked, contemplating it. *What exactly was I hoping to achieve here? What could he possibly have to say to me that could positively contribute to a single facet of my life as it currently stood?* My mouth still hadn't gotten fully to grips with smoking again; the cupid's bow crumpled uncomfortably around the butt, half-numb still, and the new tooth caps squeaked across the cotton when I sucked. Was it selfish to only want people in your life who had something worthwhile to offer you? Was I being mean, freezing him out the way that I had? I felt mean, sometimes.

The welcome mat swam up to meet me, *Dia Duit* framed with Celtic triangles on a safari-brown rectangle of mushed bristles, well worn. I turned away from it. My toes hovered on the doorstep edge. I felt mean now. Guilty. *Bad apple. Bad daughter. Bad person.* He'd stayed with me in the hospital when nobody else, not even Doireann, had shown up, and here I was, metaphorically shitting on his doorstep. I took a deep breath and pushed it all out, hard, a bluster, until my heartbeat slowed and my stomach relaxed. I stubbed my smoke out in the window box and thumbed the butt into the soil, feeling delicate roots snap under the pressure. I lifted my hand to the knocker and paused. I closed my fist tight, yellow knuckles against purpling veins, thumb across the index finger. And I tapped my knuckles on the wood instead.

Nobody answered. I stood there for another minute, almost laughing at the amount of stress I'd been under to lift my hand and knock just for nobody to be home. Then I said *fuck it* and started to leave. As I unlatched the gate, a voice called out.

—Is that you, Daughter?

I turned around and my father was standing at the side of the house, a little hobby shed open behind him, the smell of paint thinner suddenly in the air. He had a dust mask on, pulled up to his forehead like a pope's skull cap, crooked and white.

—It is.

—Jasus, only for I heard the gate latch I would have missed ya.

He came over and hugged me. I felt my spine go stiff. When he let go he led me into his house. It was cluttered but clean; so many knick-knacks filled every surface, little ceramic chickens and wrought-iron clocks and wooden signs with the Lord's Prayer on them, kitschy stuff that I never would have associated with my father. He put the kettle on and offered me a herbal tea. I nearly swallowed my tongue.

—Regular tea is fine, thanks.

—Mairead likes the herbal ones so we have a selection. I'd be more of a coffee man myself.

Mairead. I'd never met her. That was by my own design. I already had one parent who put me to the bottom of their People I Care About list. I didn't need to go through it again.

—You gave me a bit of a shock there, Daughter. Didn't expect to see you at all.

—Ah, I said I'd pop by. I wanted to say thanks again. For showing up for me with…

I gestured broadly towards my mouth.

—It's healing well enough. You wouldn't even tell. Give us a look at the new gnashers.

I bared my teeth, forgetting how to smile when it was on command. He whistled.

—Swanky. Better than mine.

He popped out his false teeth and wiggled them around like he used to when I was little, to make me screech laughing. It still worked. I laughed. It broke the weird tension. I was sick of sitting in tension with people I was supposed to love.

He gave me my mug and we went out to his shed. Now that was more of his space; it smelled like old cigarettes and pine tar, leather and methylated spirits, little pots of acrylic paint on all of the surfaces, awls and brushes and chisels and Stanley blades, dried and treated goat hides ready to be decorated and stretched onto the wooden frames of bodhráns.

—You're back to making the bodhráns?

—Oh, a long time now. Hoping to move over to this craic permanently and quit the landscaping altogether. My back is fucked. Slipped a disc laying patio slabs.

—Good market for them?

—When you run in the right circles.

I noticed the bodhráns all had painted renditions of tricolours, Easter lilies, harps, the occasional gun. One even had a black impression of Bobby Sands stamped onto its tan hide.

—Fair play.

—See that one there now? A fella commissioned that off me through Facebook. Three hundred euros profit straight into my pocket and I didn't have to lay sod for a red cent of it.

It was the Bobby Sands one. I nodded like I thought that was impressive, but I didn't know how much a regular bodhrán cost so I really had no frame of reference. I'd never heard my father's voice elevated with pride before. I was standing stock still, my hands shoved into the pockets of my coat, my breath sending dust motes swirling in the light from the open door.

—How's your mother?

—I wouldn't know. She kicked me out.

He looked worried for a split second, like I was going to ask him for something.

—It's fine. I'm living with a friend. Won't be around here too much longer anyway.

His shoulders relaxed again.

—Never mind her. She's always been a storm in a teacup. She'll forgive you.

—It's honestly fine. I'm over it.

I didn't really want her to forgive me. Being frozen out removed the guilt of being her child. But I did miss my sisters. I got a pain in my gut when I thought of them. The next time I'd see them they'd be bigger, more articulate, and probably more like Máire. It'd be harder to get along.

—That prick she married is probably worse anyway.

—JJ is actually lovely. He never gave me a hard time anyway.

—Lovely my hole. His father stole lambs from our paddock back in the spring of eighty-six and to this day that family *will not* admit it was them.

—Ah here. If you're holding onto that then you've little to be worried about.

—Not holding onto it. I just won't forget. He's still a prick.

—Alright, Dad.

He started rooting around in drawers for something before producing a small, brown rectangle.

—This is for you.

It was a handmade leather coin purse with *Saoirse* etched into it and painted in gold, a tiny crescent moon and stars beneath it. The edges were stitched together painstakingly.

I ran my fingertip over the serifs and loops of my own name and felt a swell of emotion I couldn't shove down. I wasn't supposed to shove my emotions down anymore anyway. I looked into his face. Lined with age and flecked with grey stubble. The daylight turned his eyes a shade of copper, made his pupils shrink. He was always an earnest-looking man. Capable of terrible things, and beautiful ones too. I hugged him. He patted my back gently.

—Love you.

—*Mo chroí.*

———

My mother and I both agreed that it'd be best for me to leave her home permanently as soon as possible considering the circumstances, while Doireann, who had been there during the conversation, bathing in the tension, had her phone on the counter secretly recording so I couldn't be gaslit down the line. It didn't take me too long to pack the remnants of my life in that house into a single bin bag. I'd gotten most of it out during my rage-fuelled bag-packing the night of Granny Lynch's funeral. I straightened up the room; I dusted the curtain poles, the top of the dresser, beneath the bed. I vacuumed all traces of my skin and hair from the floorboards, the skirting boards, the crevices between them. I stripped the bed bare, washed the covers myself, hung them out to dry as my mother looked on from the kitchen window.

The inside of the chest of drawers in the guest room lacked paint, bare, rough-hewn wood against neat white gloss. On impulse, I took a pair of nail scissors from my

195

bag and scratched my initials into the wood before slapping the drawer shut. Then, I ventured over to Lily's room.
Inside her music box, I hid a sheet of paper with my phone
number and email address on it, wrote that I loved her and
that I'd always answer day or night, no matter what. I also
left the Polaroid camera Charlie got me for Christmas, and
the remaining packet of film. I couldn't look at it without
feeling sorry for myself so it was best I didn't hold onto
it anymore. I still had the photo of us in Connor's shed
tucked into the back of my purse. I didn't know when I'd
throw it away. Then, I took my bin bag, shut the door to
the guest room, and descended the stairs, my boots making
loud thuds on the echoey steps. They'd already patched
and painted the drywall where my suitcase had dented it,
but it stuck out still, a small square of paint cleaner than
the rest. It gave me satisfaction to see it. I wanted to kick it
but I didn't. New Saoirse didn't do things like that. She was
above acting on petulance. Even if the *S.M.* etched on the
dresser drawer disproved that.

Doireann was waiting for me at the gap, her car idling,
staring through the gate nervously, probably anxious my
mother would appear and berate her, but Máire never left
the kitchen. She'd never let me have my own key so there
was no need for a handover, but I still froze at the front door,
like I was forgetting something. I still wanted her to want me.
I turned for the kitchen. She was staring out the window, her
back to me, her hair scraped back and tied up, her cardigan
old and wrinkled.

—What'll you tell the girls?

—I'll tell them to be anyone but you.

She'd shot to kill. I took my leave out the front, slapped the door behind me so she'd hear it, and piled the last of my crap into the boot of Doireann's Corsa before sitting into the passenger seat.

—You got everything?

—Yup. Let's blow this popsicle stand.

She took off with speed, the tyres squealing slightly, and I wound the window down and threw my middle finger up at the house, petty, hoping Máire would see it. She brought it out in me. I did not know if I would ever speak to my mother again. A serenity settled in my bones as the small, winding road opened up onto the main one, the car swallowing the tarmac, leaving nothing behind.

I'd been staying in Doireann's house for about a month as we planned our first joint foray into the adult world; she was ready to start her teaching programme and since she'd asked me to move with her, I'd been back on the employment trawl, the Dublin jobs pool exponentially wider than the one here, lots of bar work and shop work and things I had the experience to apply for now, although I'd had to lie on my CV a little bit; Doireann's phone number was now my contact for a reference from the hardware shop. She really was the best. Anyone willing to lie for you in any official capacity is somebody you don't want to let go of. I was letting myself get excited. Doireann wouldn't be starting until September but we planned to get jobs and a place to live before that, get settled into single gals life in the big city like we were in a best-friends movie, Thelma and Louise, Romy and Michele, Cher and Dionne. We'd drink espressos and smoke all the cigarettes and live on crackers and cheese while rushing from work to disco bars to parties and back, always living on the edge of something huge. When she applied for her spot in her postgrad, she encouraged me to apply for some courses too. I was twenty-four now; I wouldn't need to have good grades in my Leaving Cert to apply, just the ability to sell myself in an online application, and I'd become exceptionally versed in that. Maybe I'd study literature, or art history, or philosophy, something gentle and creative and thought-provoking, something that'd make me seem clever to all the new people we'd meet. Doireann needed a clean break from Connor, according to her, and according to me I needed a clean break from everything. I knew when I left this time, I'd never live there again. It felt good to know something with certainty. I threw some applications into all kinds of colleges and courses – politics in DCU, arts in UCD, creative writing in Trinity and Queen's and NUIG – and resolved to forget about it in case I got my hopes up.

Karen treated me like she did her own daughter. Sometimes I got overwhelmed by her kindness, her natural maternity. Doireann was her only child, not by choice; she and Paddy had tried for years before blowing all their savings on two rounds of IVF. Karen told me she'd had six miscarriages before Doireann came along. She was their miracle, proof that God could be benevolent even if he had been cruel in the past. Karen had had Doireann's name picked out for years, embroidered onto hats and baby blankets, eventually painted in big pink lettering above her cot when she knew Doireann would survive the womb. They filmed her first steps, kept her first curl and first baby tooth in little jars with ornate lids, put her first pair of shoes in a shadowbox that hung on their living room wall. She was their life, their everything. And even with all of that, they were the first ones to encourage her to go off and live her own life.

I knew it was hurting Karen to entertain the notion of an empty nest. I caught her sniffling into her sleeve more than once since Doireann had tentatively told her our Big Girl plans, wiping the face of sadness away with a hand when she caught sight of me. One morning, I found her at the kitchen table, pinewood and polished to a shine, coffee steaming. She'd just come off night shift as a healthcare assistant in the regional hospital; a thankless, shitty job that only the purest of heart could stay in for as long as she had.

—Hiya, pet. Did you sleep okay?

—Grand, thank you. How was work?

Normally not someone to divulge any lascivious details about work, the most that question ever got was a *fine* or *long* or *over now*.

—We had a woman. Stillbirth. You could hear her screaming from the hallways.

—Jesus Christ.

—He has a lot to answer for.

I got up and put two slices of bread in the toaster. I felt cold with the echo of a scream I didn't even hear bouncing around my skull. Karen's eyes were sunken into her face, hollow at the sides, tired and harrowed. Her hand lacked her rings, her Dove-of-Peace chain missing from her neck; she must have left work dazed, forgot to put them back on. When the toast popped it snapped the silence in half, made me jump. I buttered it and put it in front of Karen.

—Thank you. You're a good girleen.

I didn't know what to say. I never did when people were hurting. So I made them a hot drink or put on their favourite song or ran them a bath or buttered them some toast, little tokens, little offerings to assuage some of their pain. She patted my hand as I lifted it away from the plate.

Mothering was a complicated endeavour. Being mothered was even more complicated. It unearthed within me a trove of guilt and anger and sadness and longing, a bottomless Pandora's box of unpleasant emotion. I was starting to settle on the idea of never having children. Besides the regular struggle of being responsible for someone for two decades, I had a stab of panic at the thought of being like my own mother, in turn fucking up my own daughter, who would also have to attend therapy and avoid addictive substances and question her own suitability to be a mother, and so on. Maybe I could end that cycle with me. Maybe there didn't have to be another fucked-up Lynch descendant running endlessly into the dark nights and languishing in the auras of other people's happiness.

Karen ate her toast and went to bed. I sat in the kitchen alone, in the silence, not even a bird singing in the back garden. It was odd. I wondered where they were. Karen refilled their bird feeders with goldfinch food every week to attract all kinds of rare and beautiful little creatures. Today there was no sign. I looked out the back window. Two magpies were pulling the contents of the feeder apart and scattering the seed all over the lawn. I waved to them. *No more bad omens, please.*

———

—That dress doesn't go with the shoes.

—Don't say that. I didn't bring a backup.

—Here, swap with me.

—Ah they're a bit high in fairness, Doireann.

—They've thick heels, you'll be fine.

We were both on edge; not a sup of drink between us, Doireann on the sober train with me until we got to the pub, me on the sober train until I died probably, my nerves raw at the thought of mixing with others, rubbing off them uncomfortably with no social lubricant, my words getting lost like pebbles tossed into a stream of liquid conversation. We were currently getting ready to go out in Doireann's friend's house; a lush two-storey in one of the pricier parts of town, hidden behind a high, neat hedge with a coded gate. Her friend, Sophie, was an award-winning camogie player and a primary school teacher. She only smoked cigarettes when she was drunk and exclusively wore satin dresses to bars. She had two bichon frisés named Snowy and Poppy and would likely live in her parents' house until she married a Garda. Her hair was a waterfall. Her skin was Bermuda-tanned all year long. Her teeth were white, neat, and straight, like flattened pearls. She intimidated me just by saying hello. I would have murdered a glass of something and a line. I took off my shoes, a little strappy pair of red heels, and swapped forlornly with Doireann, pulling on her towering black velvet platforms with shaky hands. I'd been dreading this all day. All I'd managed to eat since waking up were two slices of brown toast with a scrape of Flora and now, on top of being nervous, I was starving. Doireann insisted I come. I think she felt bad about me sitting in with her parents while she went out with the gals, like I was some sort of stunted, lonely cousin she felt responsible for. I would have been more than happy to stay in and watch *Winning Streak* with Karen and Paddy. When we went down to the kitchen they were all clutching glasses and laughing at something, Taylor Swift playing on a little Bluetooth speaker on the kitchen island, everyone lovely and thin and gregarious. At the sight of me the laughing stopped and their wrists seemed to want to drop their drinks; Sophie, a gracious host, let hers hover down by her side. I wanted to kick it out of her hand. Outrage overtook anxiety and my blood was burning suddenly, chin tilting higher, spine straightening taller. *Go fuck yourselves.*

In the pub, I thought about killing myself. It kept me calm to consider the life seeping out of me from two neat, vertical lines submerged in lukewarm bathwater; easier for whoever found me to clean up afterwards. I'd never do it, of course. It was kind of like how some people think of the ocean when they're stressed. An internal oasis. If I didn't think about killing myself, I might actually have done it. Doireann was constantly elbowing me and shooting me looks like *fucking mingle for God's sake*, but that was easy for Little Miss Three Tequilas to say. The more they drank, the louder her friends got, until their previously demure laughs were loud, nasal cackles that made my fingers ball up into my hands and dig little moons into the skin of my palms. I went for cigarettes alone frequently, jacketless in the cold smoking area, clutching a flat Coke and trying not to make eye contact with people I knew in case they started talking to me. I was, however, keeping an eye out for Charlie. It'd been two months since he'd spoken to me. He'd never opened the last message I'd sent him. He'd forgotten me. I couldn't forget. It kept me awake some nights and I'd scroll back through all of our texts and read them from the very beginning and my heart would ache and ache and if I was really feeling it I'd cry, tears leaking out soundlessly and pooling underneath my right eye until I locked the phone and tried to switch my brain off, focusing on Doireann's sleep-breathing, even and meditative. She was always so steady.

She'd broken things off with Connor again that weekend; yet another girl messaged her on Instagram saying *if it was me I'd want to know* and screenshots of Connor's thirsty self begging for nudes. She'd had a little cry and a big bitching session about it before re-downloading her dating apps. I was sympathetic but tried not to be emotionally invested in them anymore; it'd only cause me trouble when they eventually got back together. Which, by the looks of things, was going to be that night. He was eyeing her from across the bar forlornly and she was tossing her hair and laughing too loud because she knew he was watching her. I couldn't take it. I got up from the table again and went to the bathroom. In the mirror I stared hard at myself until tears gathered in my lower eyelids from lack of blinking in the dry, conditioned air. I washed my hands and washed them again for good measure. I tried not to scream. Behind me, two women were sharing a stall and gossiping about an unknown third party. I started to worry it was me they were talking about and almost ran from the bathroom, face pointed towards my shoes – Doireann's shoes – and *bang*. I sent someone's pint flying, half of it on me, half of it on the floor, the smell of it overwhelming, and when I looked up, it was Charlie I had run into, and to his left, hanging from his elbow, a tiny blonde girl in a leatherette dress with a haughty expression pointed in my direction. I'd never seen her before. She was a shock. He looked like he'd seen a ghost, his empty glass rolling on the floor at our feet. I froze, wordless before mumbling *sorry*, grabbing a fistful of napkins off the bar and pushing my way back to the table. When I got there I wanted to tell Doireann what had just happened, but there was no sign of her. I asked Sophie where she was, and she just smiled and threw a thumb towards the bar where Connor was stuck to Doireann like a barnacle.

—Aren't they as cute? True love never runs smooth and all that.

I don't know if I've ever given anyone else such a withering, disgusted look before or since.

—Tell her I'm gone home. I don't feel well.

As I left the pub, I thought I could hear someone calling me back – Charlie, maybe, or probably Doireann – but I didn't stop. If I'd stopped I would have exploded, painted the walls of the pub with my brains, dramatically changing the trajectory of the lives of everyone inside, a big terrible thing flung outward instead of turned inward. I walked the town alone. It was still earlyish, nobody in the nightclubs yet. It was unfashionable to hit the clubs before midnight and loom around the dancefloor like overeager nerds. I didn't know what to do with myself, only walk on, down past all the bars and chippers and closed-up shops and unnecessary traffic lights, all set to orange because the County Council fucked up so catastrophically when installing them that it was the only solution to congestion without admitting to a mistake.

When I got to the bridge I turned down onto the canal line and stopped underneath the bridge itself, lowering myself onto the tarmac next to the canal, the tips of Doireann's heels breaking the surface tension of the dirty water like the wings of mayflies. The smell of Charlie's pint off my dress was gross. I wanted to take it off and throw it in the water. The walls of the bridge were papered with stickers and posters for mental health charities. A battered teddy and a dead bunch of roses were left at the bottom of the wall. Everyone in town knew who they were there for. The Gardaí had launched a missing person appeal and a week later he was found floating face down in the canal, tangled in reeds so overgrown that he hadn't been spotted for days. He was just the most recent. The waterways of the Midlands were popular spots for suicides. Diving boards, train tracks, fences, bridges all littered with pleas from hotlines to just give them a call instead of jumping into the cold water with stones in your pockets. The happy little stickers neglect to mention that most of these charities won't help you if you have a diagnosed disorder. You're too crazy then, even for them. They also neglect to mention that sometimes you call and nobody answers because the lines are so busy. Ask me how I know that one.

I sat there until I could hear a group of men coming up the line from the rougher side of the town. I got up and slid back the way I came when they started to smash bottles off the tarmac, hooting and laughing, and when one of them whistled to me I moved quicker still, skirting traffic to cross the road and get back to civilisation where bright lights and witnesses were abundant. *What do I do now?* I didn't want to go back to Doireann's friends. I couldn't go anywhere to be alone. I was terribly lonely. I traipsed up the town, avoiding groups of people, eyes on the footpath, arms wrapped around myself. Then I was at Gilligan's. I pushed the door open and the wall of warmth made me shiver. I was the youngest person in there by a good two decades. I sat down at the bar and ordered a vodka white. I looked at it for a while, and the barman looked at me, both waiting for me to take a drink. I carried it out to the smoking area, to be alone with it. Then I heard my father's voice, loud and runny, recounting one tale or another to whoever would listen to him. I hid behind the support beam of the plastic roofing and watched his pint wave around and around, slopping onto the table, onto his hand, his trousers. I left my drink back at the bar on my way out.

Karen and Paddy were asleep on the settee together, her head on his shoulder, an episode of *Line of Duty* put on and forgotten about. I took off Doireann's heels and silently climbed the stairs to bed. I lay down and read through mine and Charlie's messages again and again, passing out with my phone in my hand.

———

Doireann and I worked the Wednesday opening shift together every week. We had to be up and in work for a sickeningly early time, but it was made more bearable by the fact that we had to do it together. Doireann was always the first one of us up and ready to go. That's why I was incredibly confused when I was waiting at the front door with my shoes and coat on and she was still dawdling in the bathroom. Impatient and cranky from the early start, I tapped on the bathroom door and called her name.

—I don't think I'm well enough for work today.

—What? What's wrong with ya?

No answer. She was starting to panic me.

—Can you let me in?

—It's okay, just use my card and get a taxi to work.

—Or you could just unlock the door and let me in, bitch.

I heard her slide the bolt of the lock back and the door creaked open, and there she was, sitting on the bathroom floor, wan, a smell of sick in the air, clutching something in her hand. Wordlessly, she unfurled her fingers and handed it to me.

—Holy fuck.

—Shhh. The last thing I need is my mother coming down here.

I dropped my voice a few decibels.

—Sorry. But holy *fuck*.

A pregnancy test with a clear, undeniable pink plus sign in the window sat in my hand, still warm from Doireann's vice grip. I locked the door again and sat on the floor next to her. She leaned her head weakly on my shoulder, and as I stared hard at the test, stroking Doireann's hair with my free hand, in my mind's eye all of our plans – Dublin, college, new people, new jobs, new lives – burst into flame and turned to ash. Doireann's watery little voice rose up from the dampness of her chest.

—What the fuck am I going to do?

I was asking myself the same question.

VI

The Christmas Market lights were my favourite thing about Galway.

I spent a fair few of my evenings wandering in and out of the little set-ups and pathways, absorbed by the way the fairy lights turned a drab, drizzly cluster of stalls and shops into something ethereal. I bought most of my Christmas presents from the Market; handmade dolls for my sisters, a blanket for Doireann's new baby, Éabha, a set of crystalline wine goblets for Máire, thick woollen socks for my father – I felt guilty just gawking and never buying anything. If it was dry, I'd sit in one of the little coffee shed-things and drink a hot chocolate and read some more of whatever I had to read for lectures that week. I had a *lot* to read. Dense litanies of academia, essays on why *Jane Eyre* was or was not a feminist book, the effects of World War II on the writings of Samuel Beckett, the madonna/whore dichotomy of women in Ancient Greek theatre; concepts I'd not only never read into before, but things I'd never even bothered to think about. My brain was tired, but running on all cylinders nonetheless. I wanted this to work out and I was prepared to read until my eyes fell out. Plus, I *liked* it; I liked knowing new things deeply. I liked having something to be opinionated about. It made me feel more like a whole person.

My classmates were either five years younger or decades older than me, something I hadn't anticipated. Our lecture numbers were big but then we got broken down into workshop groups, and the seven other people in my group were nice enough, although I struggled to find anything in common with the younger ones; they liked to party, and I couldn't do that anymore. I'd mostly been chatty with Damien, a man in his fifties with a thick country turn to his accent, a bad knee that he couldn't keep under the desk, and small glasses that he constantly shoved back up his nose with the back of his hand. He lent me a copy of *The Dark* by John McGahern and it ruined my mood for a full week of November. I lent him my copy of *The Bell Jar* by Sylvia Plath and ruined *his* mood for a full week of November. We understood each other from then on.

Going into college still petrified me every single morning. I'd feel queasy from the minute I opened my eyes, getting ready almost catatonically, the anxiety threatening to throw me back onto the bed and pin me there. But still, I got out the door every single morning and took the bus to campus from my house-share in an estate about twenty minutes from the college. It had been gruelling to find accommodation. Firstly, because Doireann's house was significantly far away from Galway, so house viewings were a full-day affair. Secondly, because there were no fucking houses or apartments to look at that even came close to my budget. Granny Lynch's inheritance gift plus my savings would get me past December, but the education grant would never in a million years stretch to afford the rent in Galway. I had to search for a unicorn. I combed through countless scam postings and creepy men looking for female-only roommates on many, many Facebook group pages before I found two Master's students in their twenties who didn't seem like they'd cut my kidneys out and sell them while I was asleep. *Good enough.* I was ready to leave Doireann's in the last week of the summer. Doireann, on the verge of waddling, sat on her bed while I, for the third time in a year, packed my whole life into a bag and got ready to leave. I sat on the case to close it and when I looked up she was crying.

—What's wrong, you big ejit?

—I don't want you to go. If you go I'm gonna have no one to talk to but Connor.

—Sure you'll have plenty to talk about by Christmas.

That made her cry harder. I got off the suitcase and came over to pat her back while she sobbed it out. Pregnancy made her more *everything*, bigger, louder, hungrier, moodier. Her swathes of friends had dissipated fairly quickly after she announced her news. She tried to hide it, but she was hurting. Nobody wanted to hang out with someone who couldn't drink; I'd learned that lesson not long before Doireann did. I was really the only one left, but not just because of proximity. If I'd been halfway across the world, I still would have texted her every day. She was my first best friend and my last one.

Sharing her queen-size bed was starting to be a chore as she expanded outwards, only able to sleep on her side, kicking me in her half-consciousness. Connor couldn't wait to see me go so he could take my place in the house. He was moving in with Doireann and her parents instead of them getting their own place, so, in her words, they could *save for a mortgage*. I silently foretold a future where no such thing was ever going to happen. But externally, I voiced my support. She was having a whole child. That couldn't be waved away, so I couldn't be the bitch friend who hated the boyfriend. I had to be the best friend who held Doireann up, no matter who was dragging her down.

She drove me to Galway with all of my crap, despite her irascible heartburn and swollen feet. Karen hugged me fiercely on the back doorstep before I got into the car, gave me a kiss on the cheek and handed me two bags packed full of groceries that she'd bought for me. I couldn't say anything for fear of crying until we were passing the Tidy Towns sign that said *Slán! Come back soon* on the way out of town. Doireann and I took the opportunity of the journey to ignore a long goodbye and instead listened to everything we'd loved as kids; the *Twilight* movie soundtrack, McFly singles and Britney albums and stupid songs like 'Oooh Stick You' by Daphne and Celeste. The weather stayed nice, and she pulled in every forty-five minutes to let me get out of the car and smoke a cigarette. She said I could do it with the window down while we drove, that she missed the smell, but I refused; I didn't need to add smoking around a pregnant woman to my list of reasons to dislike myself.

Doireann attempted to carry some of my things into my new home. I karate-chopped her hand as it reached for my suitcase and she snatched it back, hissing.

—Don't even think about it, *compadre*.

—I'm not an invalid, you know.

—No, you're just carrying an entire human under your boobs.

She rolled her eyes and settled for lugging my new pillows up the driveway and into the house, the outer plastic crinkling and puffing as she stuffed them under her arm. My new housemates, Alex and Katerina, were inside. They already had the kettle on. Doireann shook their hands like she was my father, her car keys jangling, reminding me that yet another goodbye was on the horizon. She stayed, ostensibly for a hot drink, but really it was so she could make sure Alex and Katerina weren't really Fred and Rose West disguised as chic twenty-somethings. They were quite lovely, really. Miles more cultured than I was. Alex was doing a Master's in philosophy and Katerina was doing one in English literature. He was from Pennsylvania and she was from Gothenburg and they were quietly in love. They never kissed in front of me, but I could see it in the way they moved around one another. Cooking dinner was a dance. Sharing the sofa was an act of joy. He made her coffee every single morning and took it to her in bed. She placed a gentle hand on the back of his neck every time she walked past him in the evenings, his head bowed over the blue light of his laptop, small eyes tired behind his Harry Potter glasses. It was lovely and lonely for me at the same time.

I hadn't managed to kick the cigarettes. It was my last vice. That and occasionally a shared joint with my housemates. Alcohol and hard narcotics left my life with surprisingly little fanfare. I'd gotten drunk once since coming to Galway. I drank a bottle of wine with Katerina and Alex while we watched Hitchcock films. Grace Kelly's face started to swim around the television like koi approaching and then receding from the surface of a pond, and I excused myself for bed. I stared at myself in the bathroom mirror for a good long time. I unnerved myself. When I lay down to sleep I began crying. I picked up the phone to text Charlie and thought better of it. I made myself go to class the next morning even with the fear hanging over my head like a big dirty raincloud. I had a debilitating panic attack in a university bathroom and some random little first years patted my back and clucked gentle words at me until I could see again. I hated myself for a fortnight. I considered burning myself with many a cigarette. I settled for pressing the hot top of the lighter into my wrist over and over again. When the redness scabbed up into the shape of a Bic top, I realised how fucked up that was and scheduled a video session with Lisa-Anne. *Progress.*

The thought of having no control over myself was no longer appealing. Big girls don't relinquish control to the ether. They seize the wheel and keep themselves on the goddamned road. That's what I was trying to do. Lisa-Anne said sometimes the only closure you'll get is no closure at all. I couldn't need my mother ever again. My father, either. They were their own people, with their own issues, living their own lives. I'd have to be my own person now too. I heard from Dad only once after visiting him. He called me at three in the morning, locked drunk, half his words a jumble, the other half so sad that I couldn't even bring myself to be angry at him for waking me up. *I'm sorry, kid. I love you. Threw me out, the bitch. I'm sorry. I'm sorry.* And then radio silence. Can't expect a fish to ride a bicycle, can you?

Sometimes I still found myself so horrifically angry that I wanted to punch a hole in the fabric of space and let it suck all the matter in the universe into it, eradicating everything and everyone, myself first. But I wasn't letting myself fester in it anymore. I wasn't trying to drink or smoke or snort it away. Instead, I'd just let myself feel it, maybe throw a thump at a pillow or some other equally harmless action that might release all the tension in my hands so I didn't strangle myself or stick another lighter to myself or any other number of self-destructive things I wanted to inflict upon my own flesh. It was arse, to be honest, but it was healthier than the things I wanted to do, and that was enough for now. On particularly bitter days I considered typing up an itemised bill for my counselling sessions and sending a copy to each of my parents, just to be petty, but then the urge would pass and a reluctant empathy for them would take its place. Besides, it would make Christmas Eve a very awkward affair for the only members of my family I genuinely liked.

Lily called me one Tuesday in November. I was in the library, trying and failing to write literally even one sentence of an essay due at the end of that week, references printed, highlighted, and sprawled across the table. I wasn't used to the workload. I didn't know if I'd ever get used to it, but I'd resolved to give it a good go because otherwise I was back to being broke and uneducated. So there I was, attempting to knuckle down, something I'd never done for even one day of my life before starting college, and my phone lit up, Máire's name on the screen and my heart in my throat all of a shot. I looked around; people were giving me eyes at the sound of the vibration against the wood of the desk. I decided to answer, pressing the green button as I exited the library as quietly as I could.

—Hello?

—Hiya!

Lily's confident little voice echoed down the phone, and I relaxed. Not Máire. Just a nine-year-old with no phone of her own. Thank God. I could hear Emilia and Gracie fussing in the back of the call.

—We just wanted to ring and say we miss you and what are you doing for Christmas?

I was staying with Doireann's family who insisted I not spend the holiday alone in Galway. I wanted to be alone but I knew it was better for me not to be because I was a fucking liability when left to my own devices at times of high emotion. Even if saying yes to staying in Doireann's meant sharing my Christmas morning with Connor. The introspection thing was exhausting. I didn't want Máire to know that I was coming back yet though, and I knew she'd be just off-stage of Lily's phone call, hovering, listening, perched to snatch the phone back.

—I don't know yet. Why?

—Do ya want to come over to our house for movies and hot chocolate on Christmas Eve?

—Did your mammy say it was okay?

—Yeah, she said I could ring and ask.

—Did she now?

—She did. I swear. Do you want to talk to her?

God no. I rushed to answer.

—No, no, that's okay. I'll text her and let her know if I can make it, okay?

There was no use then in trying to write any of my essay. I trudged back into the library and shoved my things into my laptop bag, used a Tesco receipt to mark my page in *The Great Gatsby*. I'd gotten lucky with our assigned reading. I had a violent dose of butterflies on the walk home. I bought a box of cigarettes in Centra and stared long and hard at the pathetic selection of wines in the back of the shop, cordoned off by plastic grey saloon doors. I didn't buy a bottle. When I got home, Alex and Katerina were cooking a stir fry together. The house smelled like five spice and weed and chicken stuck to the wok. Kat passed me the joint over the kitchen island.

—Bad day, kiddo?

—No. Yes.

I took two pulls and handed it back to her.

—Do you wanna eat with us? We made enough for leftovers.

—Nah, it's okay. I think I'm just gonna make tea and go to bed.

I did want stir fry, but I didn't want to third-wheel. The problem with being friends with a couple was that, no matter how hard you all tried, you'd still be the gooseberry on average seventy percent of the time. I didn't have it in me. I had a tremor of panic running through me like a current, giving me a chill even in the smoky heat of the kitchen.

—Okay. We'll leave you some in the fridge anyway. And we're down to the last of the milk, it's your turn.

—Fuck, I forgot when I was in Centra. I'm sorry.

—Hey, it's only milk.

By the time I closed the door to my box room, I was crying. I'd been crying an awful lot more since I'd decided to fix my life. I'd forgotten how to compress my emotions into little bezoars that sat in the bottom of my gut for all time. Now I sprang a leak at least once a week. I thought about calling Doireann and decided not to. I knew she'd be with Éabha and Connor, enjoying their little baby bubble, and I didn't want to burst it. She'd given birth on Halloween and FaceTimed me about two hours after Éabha was born, the front-facing camera turned to the little pink squish swaddled in a hospital-issue baby blanket, her face a facsimile of Doireann's, eyes squinted and not quite adjusted to the brightness of post-uterine life.

—Look what I made.

—Welcome to the world, little bestie. Where's Connor?

I expected her to pan the camera over to a visitor's chair, Connor's legginess splayed over the plasticky leather. But she said nothing. Later on she would tell me he'd gone out drinking that evening, despite her begging him not to as she was due to drop and home alone, pains starting in the bottom of her back, her parents gone for dinner. He went anyway and turned his phone off and she stood up to use the bathroom and buckled back onto the couch with a contraction. She'd called a taxi to the hospital and pushed Éabha into the world all alone, her parents having a conniption in the waiting room because she didn't want anyone but Connor. When it was over, when the baby was out and pressed to Doireann's skin and cut from the cord and wiped down and named and loved already, he strolled into the hospital and Paddy grabbed him by the collar and strolled him back out again. Of course, they made up and were back together before they even brought Éabha home from the maternity ward. Then they were fighting again the next day when he found out I saw Éabha's face first. Then he bought her a bouquet of flowers from the petrol station and they were back on again. He was the worst. She told me her dad didn't want Connor living there anymore but what could they do? The baby was here now. She'd been having a hard time of it, even though she'd never say it. Nobody in a bad relationship wants to own up to it.

Doireann dropped me to the two monks statue. I was practising my breathing. Éabha was in the back in her little car seat, fists balled, grumbling, face screwed up. She was due a feed; Doireann's pink cotton t-shirt was sporting two dark, amorphous milk patches. She was too tired to even pull on a hoodie before she left the house, but she still came and picked me up from the bus. I really loved her.

—You look unreal. You'll be fine.

—Thanks.

—You're welcome. Now get out of the car.

—Okay.

—Saoirse. You have to open the door and get out.

—Yeah.

Eventually she leaned over and undid my seatbelt and swung the passenger door open for me.

—Go on.

I got out on Bambi legs, smoothed down my dress as I straightened up. I was wearing a cute little floral skater-skirt dress that I'd gone and bought after Charlie texted me, a pair of tights and a cardigan. My hair was tied up into an artfully messy bun that had taken almost twenty minutes to get right. I'd opted for a swipe of blush, a little mascara, some clear lip gloss. I was going for good-girl. Sober-girl. Won't-burn-down-your-life-girl. The town had the Christmas lights up, a little droopier, a little sadder than last year. I remembered the swirl of them the night I fell, how the blinking holly branches tinged my skin green as we'd waited to get into the club. My stomach pitched. I pinched the back of my hand and kept walking. The café was busy; the queue started at the door. I spotted Charlie about three people from the top. I pushed my way through to stand next to him.

—Sorry, love, the queue starts back there.

—Very funny. Hello.

—Hi. You cut your hair. It suits you.

He was just as beautiful as ever. He smelled like a car garage and aftershave mingled together. I wanted to inhale him. I wanted to run away.

—Takeaway cups and we drive to the lake?

—Go on.

At the lake, we sat in the car and looked out at the choppy surface, grey as marble, perpetually undulating, a kind of magic. The lake fascinated me. My father told me once that he and his sister used to race each other across to the lush, deciduous island in the centre, swimming from the shore, fearless of drowning. He told me that friends of his found Viking coins buried in the fertile dirt of the island, a thrill glittering up through roots and soil and loose stone. They had to be given to the National Museum of Ireland. As a child, driving to the lake was something we did weekly. We'd feed the local swans the end of bread loaves, and I'd scream at the sound of their hissing, their sharp, neon beaks ready to take the eyes out of my head. Sometimes my father would borrow a boat and take me and my mother out on the water, the rumble of the petrol engine a comfort, the smell of the fuel burning mingling with the fishy tang of lake-water. It was strange to find home in such a liminal space. When I moved away, I missed the lake more than I missed anyone or anything else. I'd already informed Doireann that if I died without warning, I wanted her to steal my body from the undertaker's and give me a Viking burial on the lake. Tie some pallets together, cover them in greenery, put me in the middle, and set me alight on the surface of the water so I could disintegrate under the open sky.

—I'm sorry I never answered the phone.

—It's okay. I wouldn't have either.

—Nah, it's not okay. I just didn't know what to do.

—Look, I'm nobody's burden.

—That's not what I'm saying.

—Why did you ask me for coffee?

—I don't know. I missed you.

—I missed you.

We weren't looking at each other. This was going to be a hardship. Lisa-Anne told me to be honest even if it felt like I was going to die of mortification. I'd never been good at telling people when they'd hurt me. I'd always been good at apologising when I hurt them though. It was easier to ingratiate myself by saying sorry all the time than to be upfront about asking for an apology. It was easier to internalise all the blame for everything that ever went wrong than to confront somebody with their own portion of responsibility. I hated to make people feel bad. I preferred to feel all the badness on their behalf. I was used to it. It was making me mentally ill.

—Are you still drinking and stuff?

—No. I'm not an alcoholic, by the way.

I wasn't. I didn't need alcohol to function. I didn't need it to do a day's work or get out of bed or talk to people. After my fall I hadn't touched a drop for nearly ten months. I knew one day I could go back to maybe a glass of wine or two at a function or a dinner. But beyond that I just didn't want to drink anymore. It didn't agree with me. It exacerbated my depression. Lisa-Anne agreed.

—I never thought you were an alcoholic. That night though, Saoirse. You embarrassed me. You embarrassed yourself. I couldn't cope with you.

—I really am sorry. But you should never have been flirting with her when you knew it'd hurt me.

The words ran together out of my mouth, liquid past my teeth, rushing into the air between us. I felt grossed out by my earnestness. It was the equivalent of sticking my fingers down my throat.

—But we weren't really together.

—Don't do that. That's bullshit.

He rubbed the back of his head with an idle hand and pressed his lips into a thin line before speaking again, a moment of irritation, the pair of us stuck sideways in it. I stared hard at the St Christopher medal hanging from his rearview mirror, silvery and still, *St Christopher Protect Us* etched into the circular frame, the man himself leaning on a big walking stick, a child on his back, safe.

—I wasn't ready for you. I wasn't ready for all of that shit. I wanted to have fun, and you seemed like fun. I never meant for things between us to get as serious as they did and you and all your long looks and your big feelings scared the shit out of me. Christ, I feel like a fucking child saying that, but it's the truth.

—So that's why you wouldn't ask me to be your girlfriend?

—I didn't ask you to be my girlfriend because I didn't want to be responsible for you.

—Ouch.

I lit a cigarette. He'd stung me with that one.

—Not to be all *boo-hoo my childhood*, but I'm trying to learn why I'm like this. I'm trying to figure out why I cling to the people I love with one hand and push them away with the other. I think it's because of my parents. Probably. Isn't it always because of them, anyway?

He looked at me, eyes all wide, and only then did I realise my mistake.

—You loved me?

—Well, I mean, yeah.

—Oh.

He drove me out to Máire's. It was quiet. The cold dregs of my tea sloshed around the takeaway cup as he took the bends, neat as a pin. I should have had him teach me to drive. I should have done a lot of things. When he pulled onto the grass verge at the end of the side road, he put his hand on my leg one last time. It sent a shiver through me like echolocation through a vast body of water. I heard it in every vestibule of my flesh. I wanted to stretch over the gear stick and kiss his mouth, his eyes, his nose, his stubble, each ear, each fine line, each pore individually. I wanted to pull him into the complex web of my nervous system. I wanted to place his heart on top of mine and have them beat in synchronicity for all time.

—What's the plan now? College and then what?

—I can honestly say that I haven't a clue.

—Well you don't seem like you're gonna come back around here.

—Probably for the best.

—I miss you like.

—Do you?

—Course. You're like the wee stray cat we used to feed.

—Pardon?

—We used to have this stray ginger cat that would sit out on the swing chair at the back of the house. Named her Bunty. Ma told me not to feed it but I kept sneaking it scraps and eventually she just lived on the swing chair. She'd drop dead shrews and birds on the back doorstep and Ma would screech murder. She left a vole in my work boot once. Right fuckin' mess when I put my foot in. I was fuming. She was just sitting in the chair looking at me like *what did you expect?* Then one morning she just… wasn't there. She never came back. We don't know what happened. But we were all gutted. Even Ma.

—So I'm like the annoying dirty cat who used to leave dead animals in your shoes?

—Don't be a dick. I thought you liked stories with morals.

I was being a dick.

—Well at least you'll know what'll happen to me. Just check my Instagram from time to time. I might be out foreign dropping mice into some fella's sandals.

—Lucky fella.

He took my right hand and kissed the back of it. He pressed it into his cheek. The stubble turned the skin pink.

I wished I could freeze us both. The goodbye was imminent. I knew I wasn't likely to really see him again. I knew something was ending but nothing felt like it was beginning. It made me want to sink to the bottom of the lake like a cinder block thrown over the side of a boat. I couldn't say it. I couldn't say the words. I was crying. His eyes were shining. He held my hand to his face for what felt like a second and a lifetime at the same time. Then he let it go. I opened the door and got out of the car. Before it closed, he leaned over.

—I think I loved you too.

The sky was growing dark, heavy with unfallen snow. I stood in the cold, wet grass and watched him disappear up the road, back to his own house probably, back to his own life, neat and regular, work then home then out then home then work. Maybe there was another girl. Good for her if there was. Nothing is permanent except transience. Things can change and be changed back again. Sometimes pain isn't decimation; it's growth. Growing hurts too. I thought my crying would escalate, but by the time his tail lights were merely red specks, my face was dry. I turned it up to the low hammock of cloud, and then towards my mother's house.

I am five years old. The roar of the petrol engine hurts my ears but I like it. My mother is holding my left hand with her right one, her wide-brimmed straw hat flapping occasionally, her floral red dress spilling off the bench, waving around her tanned, slim calves. I rest my curly little head on her bare arm and she kisses the top of my skull gently, a smile behind her puckered lips. My father is at the back of the boat, steering us out of the lake and up into the river, the reeds tall and thin, the ripples from our bow making them shiver even in the thick heat of July. His sunglasses turn amber in the sunlight and I can see the squint of his eyes as they fixate on some unseen point up the river, some destination nobody can know but him. When the river narrows he knocks the engine off and sits across from us, pumping the oars smooth as glass, the wooden edges slicing into the water, stirring it like an elixir. We pass through clouds of midges and my mother covers my face with her shawl to protect me. I wriggle free of it and lean over the boat edge to dip my hand in the cool water and my mother grips the straps of my dungarees to anchor me. Fish, slim and speedy, scatter and dart away beneath us. For the first time in my life I understand the word *happiness*. When I start school that September, the teacher will ask us to draw a picture of what we did on our summer holidays. Doireann will dig into A4 paper, a bright-pink scrawl of stick people on a beach in Spain, a pie-slice sun in the top right corner. Others will draw bouncy castles, aeroplanes, siblings, dogs, and paddling pools. I will take my crayons and draw this. Two big circles with arms and legs, and a smaller circle in between them, a nest of waxy brown spirals for hair, an upturned red parenthesis for a mouth, three full moons in a boat sailing down a river.

Acknowledgements

First and foremost, thank you to my mentor and friend Eoin McNamee, whose literary skill, measured advice and unwavering belief in the work has been nothing short of a Godsend. I owe you a pint or ten, Eoin. A huge thank you to my agent Peter Straus for advocating for me and this book from start to end, making sure it saw the light of day. Thank you to Juliet Mabey, my publisher at Oneworld, for taking a chance on *Sugartown* just when it seemed like no one else would. Your thoughtful and insightful editorial notes helped the work really shine. I'm forever in your debt. Thank you to Una Mannion for her consistent mentorship, advice and guidance from my very first day in my undergrad to now. I'm lucky to have such a talented writer and genuinely lovely person in my corner.

Thanks to everyone at RCW Literary Agency and Oneworld Publications for their hard work and support in getting this book onto shelves. You've all been so lovely and helpful and I couldn't have asked for a better debut experience. Thank you to my copy editor Tamsin Shelton who helped me polish my manuscript to perfection. I was desperate for a good red-pen edit and you did such an excellent and considerate job!

Thank you to the Arts Council for providing me with an Agility Award two years in a row, without which I wouldn't have had the time and space to (finally!) finish writing this book. I would encourage any emerging writers to apply for funding through them. A special thanks to Dr James Meaney for allowing me the use of his aunt Briena Staunton's home. The time and space was immeasurably inspirational and helpful to me, and I so appreciate it.

Thank you to my bestest, brightest, and most patient friend Orla for never letting me get swallowed by my own self-doubt, and the wonderful Siobhán for encouraging me to apply for my undergrad course all those years ago. You guys have been my biggest cheerleaders and I'm so lucky to know you both. Thank you to Fiona and Ciara whom I love and treasure regardless of the time and distance between us. Thank you to Margie for her sisterhood, and for all of those deep and insightful train talks to and from Sligo. You all were the inspiration for Saoirse's best friend Doireann, a true ride-or-die with a whip-smart sense of humour and a heart of gold. I'm blessed with all of ye!

Thank you to my family – my mother Eileen and my father Simon for creating me, for encouraging me, and for giving me a life worth writing about. My grandad Hugo and aunt Marlane for feeding my love of reading and books from the time I could string a sentence together. My wee brothers Simon and Hugh, for being a constant and much-needed source of humour, support and inspiration. Thank you to anyone in my life who had a kind word or a moment of motivation for me over the past five years. Yis are all great and I love the bones of ye.

I saved the best for last. Thank you to my fiancé and other half, Keith, for keeping me sane, alive and – most importantly – writing. You never let me quit on myself, even when I really wanted to, even when it felt like I would never write another word again. This book wouldn't exist without you, and neither would I probably. I love you, Tweedle Dum. Let's run away together. We'll bring the dog this time.